"Is that ...

Yearning bl... ...
her defensive posture. Scott came up behind her to wrap her in his arms. "The best damn deal I've ever run across," he whispered into her ear. "And the only one I've ever truly cared whether I landed or not."

Gently, he twisted her around to face him, his fingers winnowing through her hair to cradle the back of her neck, their mouths so close he could feel her breath, coming in short, sweet bursts. "And if you can't trust your intuitions, trust mine. Because they've never been wrong."

Never in her life had she wanted to believe so badly. To let herself fall into the promise in those warm brown eyes. *If this is a dream,* Christina thought, *I don't want to wake up. Ever.*

But nobody knew better than her that wanting wasn't enough to change what was.

Dear Reader,

I adore Cinderella stories, don't you? Seriously, who doesn't (at least occasionally!) fantasize about a handsome prince (or reasonable facsimile thereof) sweeping her away to a life of ease and glamour and all the cute shoes she can cram in her closet. But when the fantasy arrives for Christina Hastings—in the form of telecommunications mogul Scott Fortune—her damaged heart warns her not to trust it. Or him. So Scott has his work cut out for him, convincing Christina that he's the one who's struck it rich.

Of course most of us buy our own cute shoes. And cars. And whatever else we need. But if our princes can't exactly hand over the credit card and say, "Go for it, honey," at least they've given us their hearts—which is worth more than a closet full of shoes, any day.

Enjoy!

Karen

FORTUNE'S CINDERELLA

KAREN TEMPLETON

SPECIAL EDITION

Special thanks and acknowledgment to Karen Templeton
for her contribution to
The Fortunes of Texas: Whirlwind Romance continuity.

ISBN-13: 978-0-373-65643-1

FORTUNE'S CINDERELLA

Recycling programs
for this product may
not exist in your area.

Copyright © 2012 by Harlequin Books S.A.

www.Harlequin.com

Printed in U.S.A.

Books by Karen Templeton

KAREN TEMPLETON

Since 1998, two-time RITA® Award winner and Walden-books bestselling author Karen Templeton has written more than thirty books for Harlequin Books. A trans-planted Easterner, she now lives in New Mexico with two hideously spoiled cats and whichever of her five sons happens to be in residence.

To Marie Ferrarella,
Judy Duarte,
Nancy Robards Thompson,
Susan Crosby
and Allison Leigh,
who made my first attempt at
writing a continuity book so much fun.
And a lot less scary than I thought it would be.
We are now sisters.

Chapter One

Make it happen.

If Scott Fortune could attribute anything to his success—in life, in business—it was that simple mantra, dog-
gedly applied to every challenge that dared him to fail. Too
bad the weather on this blustery, end-of-December afternoon hadn't gotten that particular memo.

From underneath the expansive portico fronting the
main entrance to La Casa Paloma, an exclusive resort
where he, his parents and his siblings had stayed while in
Red Rock, Texas, to attend his youngest sister Wendy's
wedding to Marcos Mendoza, he glowered at the charcoal
sky. But the heavens jeered at his insignificance, the icy
rain jackhammering the battered winter lawn, the gravel
drive where a pair of SUVs waited to ferry them to the
regional airport ten miles away and the chartered jet that
would take them home to Atlanta.

"You really have to go already?"

Scott turned, smiling in spite of himself at Wendy's newly wedded—and not-so-newly pregnant—glow. Behind her, through the open, intricately carved double wooden doors, assorted family members traipsed back and forth, while the groom and his two brothers, Javier and Miguel, carted luggage out to the cars. In a minute, he'd have to herd his other siblings. But now he opened his arms to let his baby sister walk into them—as much as she could, at least—thinking that Marcos Mendoza was the luckiest, and bravest, guy in the world, taking on the family's little princess.

"You know I've got to get back," he said into his much shorter sister's slippery brown hair. "As it was, I left several projects hanging to come here."

Snorting, Wendy disentangled herself. And gently smacked his arm, her all's-right-in-her-world grin a blatant affront to the dreary weather. "Well, excuse *me* for putting you out," she said, her warm brown eyes sparkling, her accent tilting more toward Texan by the second.

"And anyway—"

"I know, I know—Daddy's hot to get back for that New Year's Eve gala y'all are sponsoring." Her mouth pulled into a pout…for about a half second before she grinned again. Wasn't that long ago, however, that those pouts had been precursors to the hissy fits of a precocious, blatantly spoiled young woman who'd assumed being an heiress *was* her life's work. At their wits' end, a year ago his parents had packed off Miss Diva-in-Training to Red Rock for some serious grounding…as a waitress in Red, the Mendoza family's restaurant. Which Marcos managed.

Poor guy probably never knew what hit him.

And neither, in all likelihood, had Wendy, who was definitely not the same wild child she'd been then. Although the marriage had been far more to get their parents off her case than to please Wendy herself, whose penchant for doing things her way was legendary. And yet, there was more to that glow than hormones, Scott suspected. She seemed genuinely happy, and content, in a way that felt almost foreign to him.

"Why don't you come see us off?" he said, suddenly loath to leave her.

Palming her burgeoning belly underneath her too-tight sweater, she shook her head. "My doctor wants me to take it easy. And to be perfectly honest—" she grinned again "—having y'all around has worn me *out*—"

"...because when people pay a thousand bucks a plate," their father said as he strode through the door, his attention far more focused on his touch-screen phone than their mother, who trailed him like an agitated, delicate gray bird, "they expect the people who got them to part with their money to show up."

Spotting her youngest daughter, Virginia Alice Fortune dragged Wendy into her arms, a small pink box containing a sampling of Wendy's exquisite desserts swung from her French-manicured fingers.

"For heaven's sake," Scott heard his mother mutter, cupping her baby's head to her cashmere-covered bosom, "it's not as if we're going to serve them their salmon and buttered asparagus personally!"

Over the crush of her mother's embrace, Wendy's eyes popped, and Scott swallowed a sigh. Because God forbid their mother—who'd raised all six of them on her own, without a nanny in sight—should stand up to their father. Not that many people did. The impenetrable aura of his vast wealth notwithstanding, at six-foot-four, his full head of dark hair barely tinged with silver, John Michael Fortune's physical presence alone made most folks think long and hard about disagreeing with him.

Which made his mother's soft, "What's the harm in staying another day or two?" all the more stunning. And finally brought his father's confused gaze to hers.

"Because I promised the Harrises we'd be there," he said, his annoyance clear. "Which you know. And it's not as if we're never coming back." His eyes shifted to Wendy, who was soon to give him his first grandchild. "Baby's due in March, you said?"

"I did."

"Then we'll be here."

But as John Michael escorted their mother to the car, Scott caught Wendy swiping a tear from her cheek. What a weird bunch they were, he mused as Marcos bounded back up the porch steps to slip an arm around his wife's thickened waist, plant a quick kiss on her lips. For as long as Scott could remember, their father had rammed home to all six of them that you were either a success or a failure—there was no middle ground…and his mother, that nothing was more important than family. Dual mantras that defined everything they did. Everything they were.

And seemed to so often be in conflict with each other.

Suddenly restless, Scott returned to the lobby, an elegant blend of terra-cotta tiles and hand-plastered walls, wrought-iron fixtures and down-cushioned leather furniture, to see what was holding up the others. In a suit and tie, his older brother Mike paced the patterned carpet in front of the registration desk, his dark brows drawn as he barked orders at whoever was on the other end of his phone, while his younger brother Blake and their sister Emily were just entering the lobby from the restaurant, deep in conversation over something on Blake's iPad screen. Only their cousin, Victoria—close to Wendy in both age and temperament—

seemed to be "in the moment," scooting toward Scott in her high-heeled suede boots, her long, dark brown curls bouncing over her shoulders.

First through the door, Victoria threw her arms around Wendy, giving her a fierce hug, then, to Marcos, a stern, "And you'd better take good care of her or there will be hell to pay," before dashing across the flagstone porch and into the waiting, rented Escalade...but not before flashing a grin at Marcos's youngest brother, Miguel, as he hefted her bag into the back.

"Guys! Let's go!" Scott called to the others. "Mom and Dad are already in the car!"

Emily, her long blond hair uncharacteristically loose, picked up the pace. "Sorry!" she said breathlessly. "But Blake just came up with this killer campaign for Universal Mobile." Her green eyes sparkling with excitement, she glanced back at Mike, who, still on his phone, was making "Yeah, yeah, I'm coming" gestures in Scott's direction, then added, "As soon as Mike closes the deal and it becomes *Fortune* Mobile."

No sooner were they outside, though, than a Jeep with *Redmond Flight School* painted on the door pulled up behind Javier's somewhat battered Explorer and a tall, cowboy-booted guy in a flight jacket and a ball cap climbed out. On seeing Tanner Redmond, Scott smiled and extended his hand, his eyes level with the other man's. Apparently a long-time friend of the Red Rock Fortunes, as well as the Mendozas, Tanner had been at the wedding... and danced, as Scott now recalled, with his sister Jordana. Who, Scott also now realized, was nowhere to be seen.

"Glad I caught you," Tanner said, his own smile glinting in his olive-green eyes as he clasped Scott's hand. "Had to go out of town right after the wedding, but wanted to say goodbye before you all left. Although..." His mouth pulled tight, the former Air Force pilot peered up at the sky, shaking his head.

Scott blew out a breath, glancing inside for his missing sister before tucking his fists in his leather jacket's front pockets. "Don't say it."

Tanner grinned again, gouging deep creases in tanned cheeks. "Who's the pilot?"

"Guy named Jack Sullivan."

"Know him well. You're in excellent hands. Man does not do stupid. Besides, this is bound to clear. Eventually."

"Thanks," Scott said drily, earning him a low chuckle and a clap on the shoulder before Tanner walked away to talk to Blake and Emily, then lean into the Escalade to pay his respects to their mother. Still one sister short, Scott asked the mob at large, "Where's Jordana—anybody know?"

"Not going," came from the doorway where his middle sister stood in plain jeans and a cowl-necked tunic, her dark blond hair pulled into her customary don't-give-a-damn ponytail. Although a brilliant asset to FortuneSouth's research and development team, Jordana clearly had not inherited his other sisters' fashion sense. Or their confidence in non-business-related situations.

Standing by the car with Tanner, their father glanced over, then lifted his own bag into the back. "Nonsense," he said, her "rebellion" clearly not worth even considering. "Of course you're going."

Jordana's arms tightened across her ribs, as something Scott couldn't remember ever seeing before flashed in her deep brown eyes. Still, her voice shook slightly when she spoke.

"I t-told you, there is no way I'm flying in this weather. Especially in some dinky little puddle jumper."

"A Learjet is hardly dinky—"

"I'm sorry, Daddy," she said, her face reddening, "but I am not getting on that plane." Even though Jordana probably racked up more air miles than the rest of them for her work, flying had always scared the crap out of her. A quirk she'd kept hidden from their father, Scott wagered. Until now. "I'll get a commercial flight later. Promise."

Smiling, Tanner said something to John Michael that Scott couldn't hear, earning him a quick glower and an even quicker nod.

"We'll expect you back tomorrow, then," their father said, then ducked into the car. Scott gave Wendy a final hug, shook Marcos's hand, then climbed into the Escalade's front seat beside Javier. As they finally got under way, he waved to Jordana, standing under the portico, hugging herself and frowning. Tanner said something to her and pointed to the still-open door. Probably suggesting they go back inside, Scott guessed, where it was warm. And dry.

"How come you're not driving your own car?" he now asked Wendy's brother-in-law.

"Like I'd miss an opportunity to get behind the wheel of this beauty?" the black-haired man said with a grin, stroking the luxury car's leather-clad steering wheel with work-roughened fingers. "No way."

Scott sighed, letting his head drop back against the headrest. "I was beginning to wonder if we'd ever get out of there," he said in a low voice, even though, between the constant swishing of the windshield wipers and both his father and brother being deep in conversation on their phones, he doubted he'd be heard.

"I feel your pain," Javier said, tossing a bright smile in Scott's direction before once more focusing on the rain-drenched road. "With three brothers, I know what it's like trying to get that many people moving in the same direction at the same time...man," he said, angling his head slightly to look up at the clouds. "At least it isn't snow, right?"

"At least."

Behind Scott, his brother laughed. A calculated *We're all friends here, right?* laugh designed to put the other party at ease. A tactic Scott had mastered before his twenty-fifth birthday—

"You worried about your sister?"

The unexpected question sliced through Scott's thoughts. "What? Oh. No. Not at all. I—we—can tell, Wendy couldn't have done better than with your brother. I get the feeling he'll be very good for her."

Javier chuckled. "Think maybe it's the other way around, to be honest. Dude needed some serious shaking up. And Wendy was just the girl to do that. But I wasn't talking about her. I meant the one who stayed behind. Jordana, right?"

Scott frowned. "Worried? No. Jordana's a smart cookie."

"No doubt. But…maybe a little shy? At least, next to Wendy…"

A half smile tugged at Scott's mouth. "*Everybody's* shy compared with Wendy. But then, more than one Wendy in the family might have taken us all under. So, I hear you're a developer…?"

They fell into an easy conversation for the next few miles, everyone's chatter competing with the hammering of rain on the Escalade's roof, the windshield wipers' rhythmic groans. When the visibility worsened, however, Javier became far more intent on driving than talking, giving Scott a chance to check his own messages on his iPhone. Not that there were many this close to New Year's, but the business world never completely stopped, even for the holidays.

He heard his mother ask his father something, his father's curt, distracted reply. A relationship dynamic he'd always taken for granted...until witnessing Wendy and Marcos together.

As far as he could tell, the relationship his sister and new brother-in-law had seemed to be based on mutual regard and respect for each other's opinions and intelligence. God knew, he thought with a smile, his strong-willed sister was not easy to live with, but Marcos seemed to actually thrive on the challenge. The stimulation. And while Wendy would never be "tamed" by any stretch of the imagination, being with Marcos had obviously forced her to focus on something other than herself. And that could only be a good thing.

Which made Scott wonder—not for the first time, as it happened—what, exactly, had kept his parents married for more than thirty-five years. Loyalty? Habit? After all, it was no secret—at least to their children—that the relationship was strained. Strike that: it might be a secret to his father. Because as Virginia Alice's role as mother became more and more attenuated, Scott more and more often caught the haunted "Now what?" look in her eyes.

And yet, Scott had no doubt their bond was indissoluble, if for no other reason than appearances meant too much to both of them. Lousy reason to stay together, if you asked him. And why, in all likelihood, their older progeny sucked at personal relationships. Business savvy? The drive to succeed? Sure. Those, they all had in spades. But the ability to form a lasting attachment to another human being?

Not so much.

Scott exhaled, thinking of his own track record in that department. Granted, his lack of commitment was by choice. He enjoyed the company of women, certainly, but falling in love had never been on his agenda. Or in his nature, most likely.

Which was why seeing Wendy so...*blissful* was...unsettling. As though she hailed from a different gene pool altogether. Cripes, she was so young. So fearless, falling in love with the same reckless abandon as she did everything else—

His phone rang, rescuing him from pointless musings.

"Scott Fortune here—"

"Mr. Fortune, glad I caught you. It's Jack Sullivan. Your pilot?"

"Oh, yes... What can I do for you?"

He heard a dry, humorless laugh on the other end of the line. "Not a whole lot, I don't imagine. Afraid I've got some bad news—all this rain's flooded out the route I normally take to the airport." At Scott's muttered curse, the pilot said, "Oh, I'll be there, don't you worry. Just gonna take a bit longer than I'd figured."

"How much longer are we talking?"

"Hard to say. Might be a half hour or so, maybe a little more. But until this weather straightens out I'm not taking that bird up, anyway. So y'all just go on ahead and sit tight, have a cup of coffee, and hopefully this will have all blown over by the time I get there. Good news is, hundred miles east of here, it's completely clear!"

"Problem?" Mike asked quietly behind him. His brother's thinly veiled criticism made Scott bristle, as it always had. Not that he'd take the bait.

"Pilot's going to be late," he said mildly, slipping the phone back into his pocket. "Roads are flooded." At Mike's soft snort, he added, "Hard as this might be to believe, there are some things even *we* can't control."

As if on cue, they hit a squall that was like going through a car wash, making Javier slow the car to a crawl and Scott's mother suck in a worried breath.

"Man," Javier said. "I sure wouldn't want to fly in this

weather. I'm beginning to think your sister had the right idea, staying put."

Probably, but despite what he'd said to his brother, Scott was chafing, too, at their plans being derailed, at being in a situation over which he was powerless.

Because first, last and foremost, he was a Fortune, and Fortunes did not like being told "no."

Ever.

From behind the snack bar counter, Christina Hastings watched the well-heeled group trickle through the front door and across the tiled lobby of the chichi private airport and reminded herself of two things: one, that being envious was a waste of time and energy; and two, that being grateful for what you already had went a long way toward receiving more.

And besides, she had goals. Because a girl had to have goals, or she might as well shrivel up and die.

Sighing, she tossed her long braid over her shoulder, then checked the coffeepot to make sure it was still full, casting a baleful glance toward the two-story window running the full length of the lobby's back wall. It was dumb, letting the gloomy weather get to her. Dumber still that she'd agreed to come in on her day off, in case somebody had a sudden hankering for a premade Caesar salad with three bites of chicken or an overpriced bottle of water. By rights, she should be home, wrapped up in a throw on her sofa with her dog, Gumbo, smooshed up beside her, watching *Buffy* DVDs and enjoying the next-to-last day with her little fake Christmas tree before she took it down for another year.

Instead, she was amusing herself—although she used the term loosely—by watching the goings-on in front of her. Living in Red Rock—as opposed to under one—it had been impossible not to hear about the Fortune/Mendoza wedding at Red, the local family restaurant in town she'd only ever seen from the outside. Or that the small jet still in its hangar on the other side of the flight school building had been chartered to take the bride's family back to Atlanta. Not that it apparently mattered whether the men— all tall, all dark, all handsome, sheesh—were here, there or in Iceland, given their preoccupation with their spiffy, and probably five-minutes-old, electronic toys. As opposed to her ancient flip phone with half the numbers rubbed off. Made texting a mite tricky.

Not that she had anybody to text. She was just saying.

"Hey, there. What's good today?"

She smiled for the improbably red-headed flight attendant she'd seen once or twice before, dressed in a nondescript uniform of black pants and vest over a long-sleeved white shirt. "Same as always. Although the turkey sandwiches don't look half bad."

"Let me have one of those, then. And a Diet Coke."

"You flying out with this group?"

"Yep. The Atlanta branch of the Fortunes. Older guy's the father, the younger men his sons." As the flight attendant waited for her order, she nodded at the women now gathering in the posh lounge tucked underneath the second-floor offices on the other side of the lobby. "Not sure about the women, though. Although the little blonde looks exactly like the older one near to having a conniption, so I'm gonna guess she's a daughter." She pulled the tab on her soda. "Wonder what's got Mrs. Fortune so bent out of shape?"

She was, too. Elegant, reed-thin, the still-beautiful, silver-haired woman periodically pressed a tissue to her mouth, while the conservatively dressed blonde tried—with little success, it seemed to Christina—to comfort her distraught mama. A third woman—younger than the others, very pretty, oblivious to what was going on around her—flounced past them to plop down on one of the sofas. She leaned over to tug an e-reader out of her giant designer purse, her long, dark curls spilling over the shoulder of her cropped suede jacket, which matched her killer boots.

As the attendant droned on about the weather, Christina watched the Fortune brothers—one dressed like he was about to meet the president, another in a sportcoat and jeans, the third decked out in a wicked cool leather jacket and black pants—milling about, each in his own little world. Close in age, looked like. Lord, no wonder the older woman was distraught—she was awfully skinny to have pushed out that many kids that close together. A thought that evinced a brief pang Christina had no intention of indulging.

She handed the attendant her change; the redhead thanked her, then left to go talk with Mrs. Fortune. The brunette, apparently too fidgety to stay seated, got up to wander aimlessly into the lobby to look at a glassed-in display of model planes in the middle of the floor. A second later some guy in a cowboy hat strode past, carrying a stack of boxes…and winked at the brunette, obviously startling her into scurrying back into the lounge, where the oldest of the men and one of the younger ones had settled into opposite ends of the biggest sofa, yakking on their phones and ignoring the excited weatherman trying to get their attention on the big-screen TV.

Two more handsome young men ferried inordinate amounts of luggage into the building, piling it near the exit to the airfield. One lobbed a quick smile in Christina's direction before heading back outside. The highlight of her day, she thought morosely, only to mentally smack herself.

Overhead, thunder complained as the skies poured even

more rain across the glass wall, hard enough to nearly obliterate the small single-engine plane on the other side—

"Excuse me? Could I get an espresso, please?"

With a start, Christina jerked around, running into a pair of bronze-ish eyes. Ah. The One in the Leather Jacket. The *pissed* One in the Leather Jacket, apparently.

Christina shrugged, apologetic. Tried unsuccessfully to ignore the mouth. And the cheekbones. Holy moly. Not only did this family have, if the scuttlebutt was to be believed, more money than God, they had a gene pool to die for. "Sorry, all I've got is regular. Or decaf."

"You're not serious?"

Okay, the man was easily the best-looking guy she'd ever seen in her entire life—how she wasn't blinded, she did not know—but still. A pain in the butt is a pain in the butt.

This ain't Starbucks, Bucko, she wanted to say. But she didn't. Partly because she didn't have the energy, and partly because, along with his iPad, the guy was toting a silly little pink bakery box. Which for some reason tickled her no end.

"For what it's worth," she said, "which isn't much, I'll grant you, I've been after my boss to get an espresso machine ever since I started working here. He ignores me. So." Overhead, hail pummeled the steel roof, the sudden din making her jump. Outside it looked like God had dumped out His snowcone machine. When she turned back to Leather Jacket Dude, he was glaring at the deluge.

"It'll let up," she shouted over the barrage. Although why she felt compelled to reassure him, she had no idea. He turned the glare on her, and she sighed. "Regular or decaf?"

The man grimaced. And he hadn't even tasted the coffee

yet. Forget an espresso maker, Christina couldn't even get
Jimmy to spring for a decent Colombian brew.

"Regular," he grumbled. "Black."

Christina opened her mouth, then shut it again, thinking *Just give the man his coffee, honey chile.* She poured
it into a foam cup, smooshed a plastic lid on top, then set it
on the black granite counter, wiping her hands on the seat
of her jeans to keep from messing up her apron, which was
a bear to get clean. "That'll be a dollar fifty. The flight attendant said you're all family?"

He barely glanced at her before reaching inside his
jacket for his wallet, the slight move releasing a very pleasant scent. Probably not something he picked up at Wal-
greens. "Yes. We were here for my sister's wedding."

"Oh, that's nice. From Atlanta, right?"

He frowned slightly, like he couldn't figure out why
on earth she was talking to him. Well, tough. Talking to
people was what kept her from going insane, giving in
to the loneliness that sometimes felt like it would suffo-
cate her. Gumbo was a great dog, but his conversational
skills were limited. "Yes," he said, looking up when the
hail stopped, as abruptly as it had started.

"See?" Christina said. "Told ya. You watch, the sun'll
be out before you know it."

For a moment their gazes touched, his a bit disconcerted
as his cell phone rang. Almost like he heard the distinct
twannnnng in Christina's midsection. Uh-oh. Distractedly
he hunched it to his shoulder, mumbling, "Scott Fortune,"
as he handed her a twenty, then started to walk away.

Must be nice, she thought as the twanging died out, to
be able to treat twenties like quarters. "Wait! You forgot
your change—"

A deafening, blood-chilling roar drowned out her words,

raised the hairs on her arms. Scott turned, the startled look in his eyes tangling with hers a split second before the glass wall exploded and Hell rained down around them.

Chapter Two

The woman's scream pierced his brain, rudely dragging Scott back to consciousness. His heart pounding hard enough to hurt, he lay motionless, his eyes still closed, his ears still ringing, trying to regain his bearings...until she screamed again.

"For the love of all that's holy, *stop that*."

After a beat or two of blessed silence, he heard, "I thought you were dead."

That raspy voice...ah. The waitress. "No. At least I don't think so—" The last word ended in a cough; yanking his jacket collar over his mouth and nose, Scott opened his eyes. Panic cramped his chest: through the occasional shaft of dust-clogged light eking through the rubble, he realized he'd come damn close to being buried alive. He fumbled for his phone, only to realize it had apparently fallen out of his pocket. Damn.

"Um, are you okay?" she said. "I mean, c-can you help me? I'm stuck."

Adrenaline spiked through him. "Hold on..." Debris clattered as Scott tried to heave himself upright, only getting as far as his knees when his right temple gave him hell. Flinching, he quickly brushed his fingers over the spot—no blood, thank God. "Where are you?"

"Close enough to think you were dead, obviously. I can see you, though. Kinda. Keep going, you'll find me."

"How long was I out?" he asked as he cautiously crept toward her.

"Not long. Couple minutes, maybe? You remember the tornado hitting?" she asked when he reached her, barely six feet away. Propped on her elbows, she lay back against what he assumed was the counter base, her legs imprisoned beneath a pile of rubble. Even through the haze he could see the grim set to her mouth.

"Yes," Scott said quietly, knowing he'd never forget the wind's brutal, relentless shrieking, like a million furious demons. "Guess I blacked out right after, though. Does it hurt?"

"I don't think...no. Not really. Not sure if that's a good thing or not. I can't move, but at least I don't feel like I'm being crushed. But something—" Grimacing, she strained to pull herself free; Scott's hand shot to her shoulder, stopping her.

"Stay still. Do you hear me?"

Not looking at him, she nodded. "Just...hurry."

"On it," he muttered as he snatched away the lighter stuff—wood lathing, plaster chunks, shards of glass. But despite having lifted weights for years, Scott was no match for the granite slab pinning her to the ground. He tried another angle, his back and shoulder muscles burning like a sonuvabitch, but no dice. Sitting back beside her, he punched out an exasperated breath. "Why the hell did they use granite for the counter?"

Her head fell back, her eyes shut. "And yet," she said through faint, rapid breaths, "no espresso maker. Go figure."

More dust sifted down beside them, the sound like scurrying ants. "Call me crazy, but this seems like an odd time to crack jokes."

"It's that or s-scream again. D-deal."

He groped for her hand in the dim light, found it; her fingers tightened around his, kicking his heart into overdrive. "Take some deep breaths before you hyperventilate. There, that's better," he said when she complied, then gently squeezed her hand. "You scared?"

A snort preceded, "Yeah, fear is kinda my go-to emotion when I think I might die."

"We're not going to die."

"Oh? Last I heard, death couldn't be bought off."

"What's that supposed to mean?"

Her eyes opened as she shifted, clearly trying to suppress a wince. And shivering. "S-sorry. Today hasn't gone exactly the way I thought it w-would...no, it's okay, I'm fine," she said when he let go to shrug off his jacket.

"I'm wearing a sweater. You're not. So no arguments. Can you sit up a little more?" Nodding, she did, at least enough for him to wrap the jacket around her shoulders, tug her smooth blond braid free.

"Thank you."

"Anytime." Elbowing aside the first stirrings of alarm, Scott glanced around. "This is...surreal."

"Yeah," she said. "Especially as I can't recall ever seeing a tornado around here before. Farther north and west, sure. But..." Her eyes lifted. "I think...I'm gonna pretend this is all a dream. And any minute I'll wake up and...it'll be over."

"Sounds like a plan." He inched a little closer. "I'm Scott, by the way."

"I know." Her eyes drifted closed again. "Heard you on your cell phone."

"Speaking of which, mine's gone AWOL. Do you have one?"

"Sure thing. In my purse."

"Which is where?"

She almost laughed. A sound that, under other circumstances, he would have found extremely appealing. "Around here somewhere. And you need to be quiet now."

Scott angled his head to see into her face. Her eyes were still shut. "You didn't tell me your name."

"Christina. Hastings. Now hush."

"What…what are you doing?"

"Praying. Trying to, anyway."

"You really think that'll help?"

"We'll never find out if you keep talking, will we?"

A damp draft swept through their little cave. "Is your head okay?"

"And that better not be you thinking I'm off my nut because I'm praying."

He did, but he wasn't about to say that. "Not at all. But if your head got hit, you might have a concussion. So you shouldn't close your eyes in case you fall asleep."

"Oh. No. Head's fine. Well, no worse than usual—"

A muffled sound from outside made Scott jump. Holy hell. How could he have forgotten—?

The initial shock sloughed off, he jolted to his knees again to claw at the wall of debris barely three feet away separating him from the others. "Blake! Mike!" He yanked at a chunk of drywall, sending plaster dust and small

chunks of heaven knew what sifting down on them. "*Dad!*
Can you hear me—?"

"For heaven's sake, stop!" Christina snapped behind
him. "You want to bring whatever's left up there down on
our heads?"

"No, but…*dammit!*" Terror erupting in his chest, he
stared into the darkness quickly swallowing up what might
as well have been a mountain. "Most of my family's out
there. Somewhere."

"It'll be okay," she murmured, although he wasn't sure
if the reassurance was aimed at him or she was trying to
talk herself down off the ledge. Scott duckwalked back to
where she lay, planting his butt on the floor beside her and
listening to the unremitting drip, drip, drip of rain somewhere above them.

"You sure about that?"

A beat passed before she said, "Somebody's bound to
know what happened, where we are. It might take a while,
but…we'll be okay."

He could barely see her now, but that first image when
he'd looked up from his phone earlier and actually *noticed*
her was indelibly etched into his brain: the sass and intelligence in those enormous blue eyes, the barely repressed
humor—at his expense, no doubt—behind her smile. "For
somebody convinced a minute ago we were about to die,
you seem amazingly calm now."

"I had my moment. It's over. Or I could be in shock.
Hard to tell."

"Or maybe you did get beaned."

Her soft laugh melted something inside him. "Or maybe
I did."

Crazy. Most women he knew would be in hysterics by
now. And Christina's hair and skin had to be as caked with
plaster dust as his, her eyes and mouth as gritty. Not to

mention she couldn't have been more than five-two, five-three tops. And yet—

"You're tougher than you look."

"So I've been told."

More distorted sounds from the other side of the wall snagged his attention; he crawled over, shouting. "We're in here! Can anybody hear me? Javier! Is that you?"

"You're wasting your energy, you realize."

His head swung back to her. "I can't sit here and do *nothing.*"

"Looks like you don't have much of a choice."

"Doing nothing is not a choice."

"We're not doing nothing. We're waiting." She paused. "And trusting."

"Ah. That praying thing again, right?"

He sensed more than saw her shrug before she said, "Tell me about them. Your family."

"Why?"

"Maybe it'll keep us distracted."

Scott's gut contracted. "You *are* in pain."

"Let's just say I'll never complain about cramps again."

Honestly. "Do you always say whatever pops into your head?"

"Depends on the situation. This definitely qualifies. Besides…" She shifted slightly. "Either we're gonna die, in which case we'll never see each other again. Or we'll be rescued—which would definitely be my preference—and you'll go back to Atlanta, and we'll still never see each other again. Either way, I'm not too worried about making a good impression."

Except you are, Scott thought, startled, thinking if he had to be trapped in a pile of rubble with anybody, he could have done far worse than this smart-mouthed, cool-as-acucumber little bit of a thing with her soft, raspy voice and even softer blue eyes.

"So talk," she said. "How many of you are there, exactly...?"

He made her laugh.

And, bless him, forget. As much as she could, she supposed, given the situation. But considering their initial encounter, not to mention the frown lines he'd probably been working on since kindergarten, the last thing Christina had expected was for the man to have a sense of humor.

Not that she couldn't hear weightier threads lacing the stories about growing up with five siblings, despite Scott's obvious discretion at how he presented his family to a complete stranger. Even so, when, for instance, he told her some silly story about him and his older brother, Mike, setting up competing lemonade stands across the street from each other when they were kids, she could hear the frustration—and hurt—underlying his words. Mike couldn't let an opportunity pass to one-up his younger brother...and that their father had praised eleven-year-old Mike for his ingenuity at besting Scott, who'd only been in the third grade at the time.

She was also guessing that Scott had been busting his buns trying to win his father's approval ever since. Not that Scott would ever admit as much—certainly not to Christina, at least—but nobody knew better than she did what it was like to yearn for a parent's attention and respect.

His obvious loyalty—and genuine affection—was honorable. But good Lord, if half of what he'd said was true, this family took the concept of sibling rivalry to new heights, not only not discouraging competition but fostering it, pitting the kids against each other to make them stronger. More fierce. And yet, from what she could tell, they all loved each other, even if those bonds were mainly forged by their mutual interest in FortuneSouth's success.

It was enough to almost make her grateful she was an only child.

"So what do y'all do for fun?" she asked.

"Fun?"

It was almost totally dark by now. And cold. Cold enough that they leaned into each other for warmth. And comfort. The pain in her leg and foot had settled into a dull but constant ache. As had the fear, which was almost like a third person in the space.

"It's not a trick question, you know."

"More than you might think," Scott muttered, then parried, "What do *you* do for…fun?"

"I asked you first."

He blew out a heavy sigh, his breath warm in her hair. "Okay…we…go to a lot of charity events." His accent was pure Southern-privileged, his voice pure man, all low and rumbly. A delicious, and deadly, combination. "Dinners, that sort of thing."

"Sounds boring."

"Excruciatingly."

"For pity's sake—I said *fun,* Scott. Or do you need me to define the word?"

"How would you define it?"

"Well…fun is something that makes you feel good. Makes you happy. Makes you glad to simply be alive."

"Such as?"

She thought. "Goin' to the state fair and eating your weight in fried food. And cotton candy. Tossing burgers on the grill on a summer night, sittin' around and chewing the fat with friends. Driving to nowhere with the top down, stopping wherever you feel like it. Sittin' on the steps and watching fireflies. What?"

"Apparently your definition of *fun* doesn't include the word *exciting*."

"Does yours?"

"Good point."

"I said, it just has to make you feel good."

"So…is that your life? In a nutshell? Going to the fair and chowing down on burgers and watching fireflies?"

After a long moment, she said, "I said that's how I define fun. I didn't necessarily say that was my life. Not at the moment, anyway."

"That doesn't sound good."

"No, it's okay. I'm just…I'm kind of…focused on other things right now." When he got real quiet, she said, "What are you thinking about?"

"That I've never been to a state fair."

"Get out."

"It's true. But also…that I can't remember the last time I felt good about doing something that didn't involve improving the bottom line."

"And *that* is too sad for words."

"There's nothing wrong with making money, Christina. FortuneSouth provides jobs for thousands of people—"

"Oh, don't go getting defensive. I never said there was anything wrong with making money. But you have to admit there's something off about only getting your jollies from work."

Another pause. Then: "I don't *only* get my jollies from work."

"Lord, I can practically hear your brows waggling. And *that* doesn't count," she said when he laughed.

"It doesn't?"

"Not that it can't be fun—don't get me wrong. But it's so…trite."

Scott barked out a laugh. "Point to you."

"Thank you."

She felt him shift beside her. "You remind me a little of my youngest sister. Wendy."

"The one your parents sent out here because she was about to drive 'em up a wall?"

"The very one."

"Is Wendy your favorite?"

"Yes. But don't you dare tell her that. Or anyone else."

"Your secret's safe with me." Christina thought a moment, then said, "I'm very flattered, then."

Scott chuckled. "So tell me about *your* family."

Yeah, he would ask that. "Not a whole lot to tell. My father jumped ship when I was a toddler, never to be seen again, and my mother…we're not real close."

"I'm sorry."

"Yeah. Me, too."

"No brothers or sisters?"

"Nope. But I do have a dog…ohmigosh!"

"What?"

"I can't believe I forgot! *I have a dog.* And I have no idea if he's okay—"

Feeling her eyes burn, Christina pressed a hand to her mouth. Not being dead yet, she figured she was ahead of the game, but suddenly not having any idea how her baby was made her sick to her stomach.

"What's his name?" Scott said gently.

She lowered her hand. "G-gumbo. 'Cause when God made him he tossed whatever parts He had on hand into a bowl, and Gumbo was the result. Although he gets called Dumbo a lot, too," she said on a shaky little laugh. "Dog's dumber than a load of bricks, I swear. But he's mine, and I love him, and—"

The tears came whether she wanted them to or not. The shock came when Scott slipped his arm around her shoulders and pulled her head to his chest. Not saying anything, just holding her close.

So. Unfair.

Then her stomach rumbled. "How long do you suppose we've been here?"

"I have no idea. It's been dark for a while, though."

She listened. "Rain's stopped."

"Yep. In fact, there must be a full moon."

Christina blinked, noticed the silvery light here and there delineating the scene. "Oh, yeah." She sighed. "I'd kill for a burger and fries right now."

Another of those low chuckles preceded, "You and me both."

"While we have the light…there's a refrigerated case, if you can get to it, with food, such as it is. And water and stuff."

"Be right back."

He disappeared; for several minutes she heard scuffling, some cursing. Then a surprised, "I'll be damned. I found my phone. Although…crap. No service. But…hold on…"

A minute later he returned with a couple of sandwiches, two bottles of water and that little box. "The case was pretty banged up," he said, sitting beside her again. "But still cold. I have no idea what I got, though."

"Ask me if I care," she said, grabbing one of the sandwiches and ripping off the cellophane. "So what's in the box?"

"Heaven. Or so I'm told."

"Yeah?"

"Yep. After she started working at Red, Wendy discovered she had a talent for making desserts. So she gave all of us a sampling of some of her creations." He turned on his phone, the feeble light illuminating the contents of the box enough for Christina to see several kinds of cookies, some sort of bar thing and a Napoleon-like pastry. "Help yourself, I'm not big on sweets. But you'd better believe I wouldn't tell Wendy that."

The sandwich gone, Christina hesitated, then selected something that melted in her mouth. Butter and chocolate and caramel and maybe some kind of liqueur? It was the fanciest thing she'd ever tasted in her life, given that, for her, a "splurge" was buying real Oreos instead of the Walmart fakeouts. Which *she* wasn't about to tell *Scott*.

"That was amazing" was all she said, then closed the lid on the box.

"Please. I mean it. Take what you want."

Like she'd ever been able to do that in her entire life. "No, it's okay. I'm good."

Their meal done, they sat in silence for a little while, digesting what had happened to them—well, at least that's what Christina was doing—as well as their food. Outside, the wind had picked up enough to whistle through the jagged orifices left in the wake of the destruction. Close by, something periodically scraped against the wall on the far side of what used to be the snack bar.

Scott cleared his throat. "I think we need to keep talking—"

"Yeah, I think you're right. Absolutely." Then she yawned. "If I can stay awake. I think the adrenaline's gone."

"You comfortable?"

"I've been better. Been worse, too."

He pulled her close again. "Lay your head on my chest."

"I couldn't—"

"One, you already have. And two, I cannot tell you how little I'm in the mood for arguments right now. And I'm cold, too. So just do it, dammit."

All righty, then. Although, even before her cheek made

contact with his soft, soft sweater—and the hard, hard muscles underneath, Christina knew she was doomed.

Whether they made it out alive or not.

Scott couldn't remember the last time he'd held a woman close—one not related to him, that is—with no ulterior motive in mind. Or when doing so had provoked such mind-blowing feelings of…tenderness. Especially when, with a long sigh, Christina relaxed against him.

"Better?"

"Yes, actually." She lightly rubbed his chest. Probably not the best move. "What is this stuff? Cashmere?"

"Silk and lambswool. Wendy gave it to me for Christmas."

Her hand once more fisted near her chin, she said, "Gal's got good taste."

"That she does." Fingering her shoulder, he asked, "So tell me—who is Christina Hastings when she's not pawning off lousy coffee in an airport?"

A little laugh preceded, "You tasted it, then?"

"Unfortunately, yes. Well? What are your dreams?"

"Now why on earth would you be interested in my dreams?"

"Would you rather talk about sports? Politics?"

"God, no."

"Good. Because neither would I." He paused, then added, "I don't make small talk, Christina. Or ask questions I don't really want answers to. And we agreed we need to keep talking—"

"Okay, fine. Short term or long term?"

"Either. Both."

"Well, first, to finish getting my business degree. Although I've been working on that one for some time already. I didn't…I got sidetracked after I finished high school, so I didn't start college until I was twenty-one. And even then I've always had to work while going to school, so I've only been able to take a couple courses a semester. I'm definitely a tortoise and not a hare."

"Nothing wrong with that. But there's no one to help you out?"

"Not really, no. Although I'm hoping to finish up in the next year or so. And after that—*way* after that, most likely—I'd like to have my own business."

"Doing what?"

"You don't—"

"Christina. Captive audience. Go for it."

A moment passed before she said, "I've got a couple of ideas, although nothing's set in stone. But I'm good with animals, so I thought maybe a pet grooming shop. Or one of those spas where people could leave their pets for me to spoil while they go on vacation? Although that would mean owning someplace large enough to do that, so that's definitely on the 'someday' list...oh, it's silly, isn't it?"

"Now why would you say that?"

"Because...I don't know. My plans must seem like small potatoes to somebody like you."

"One, you are not allowed to sell yourself short. Two, all businesses start with a seed. An idea. Feed that idea with focus and determination and it will grow."

"And sufficient start-up capital," she said with a sigh.

"Somebody's done her homework. I'm impressed."

"Homework, I can do. Finding money lying around under rocks, not so much."

He smiled. "If the idea is good, the financing will fall into place."

"So would *you* finance my start-up?"

"Cheeky little thing, aren't you?"

"So would you?"

Scott chuckled. And got a sweet whiff of what was left of her perfume or hair stuff or whatever it was. "Show me a well-thought-out business plan and we'll talk."

"You're not just saying that because you're figuring we're gonna die here and then you'll be off the hook?"

"We're not going to die, Christina."

She snuggled closer, her arm banding his ribs as she whispered, "Do you know I've never told another living soul about this?"

"Not even your mother?"

"Especially not my mother." She paused. "Since she's shot down everything I've ever tried. Or ever wanted to do. Not exactly a big cheerleader."

"That's rough."

"Eh," she said on a shrug, "it taught me early on to be self-reliant. 'Course, that doesn't make an ideal mate, either. Prob'ly why I haven't been on a date in, oh…two years?"

Gal was definitely getting tired, Scott thought with a weary smile of his own. Inhibitions shattered and all that.

"Two years? Really?"

"Yep." She yawned. "Got tired of the stupid games. Of meeting a guy and thinking he's nice, only to find out he automatically expects something in return for taking me out to dinner. That he's not even remotely interested in getting to know me as a person. Sucked."

Bitterness, dulled and worn, veneered her words. And provoked him into defending his sex. "Not all men are like that."

"Then maybe I'm just lousy at picking 'em," she said, her accent getting heavier the sleepier she got. "But you know? I'm okay with being on my own. It's kinda nice, being able to make my own decisions about what's best for me without having to swing 'em past anybody else."

This last bit was accentuated with a sweeping arm gesture before she snuggled closer, rubbing her cheek against his chest. Damn.

"You're awfully young to be so cynical," he said into her dusty hair.

She shrugged, clearly unperturbed. "Better than havin' my head in the clouds."

She yawned again, one of those double yawns that signified that sleep couldn't be far behind. Yet despite her soft voice, her words were clear. "I'm a realist, Scott. I know who I am. Where I came from. Maybe not exactly where I'm going, but close enough. What's in my control and what's not. Like…if I never get married, maybe I'll… adopt someday." She hmmphed tiredly. "Never told anybody *that,* either."

And the longer she talked, the more her honesty seemed to wrap around his soul, nourishing something inside him he hadn't even known was hungry. "Were you always this wise? Or has experience made you this way?"

"Hell if I know," she said, and he laughed. "But I am a real firm believer in being true to yourself. In knowing who you are and what you want, and then doing your best to make those two things work together. Long as you understand the road between points A and Z might not always be a smooth one."

At that, Scott held her closer, resting his cheek in her hair, as if doing so would help him absorb some of whatever it was that had so firmly grounded her. "What if…you get so entrenched in Point A you can't even see Point Z? What if you're not even sure what Point Z is?"

He could sense her tilting back to look at him, even though he couldn't imagine what she'd see in the murky light. "Seems to me all you need to know is that where you are in your life? It's not working anymore. And then have the guts to do something about it. Because way too many people get so caught up in doing things the way they've always done them, living the lives they've always lived, that they don't even know they're unhappy. And that, to me, feels unbearably sad."

She molded herself to him once more, as though she belonged there. "I don't want to die with regrets, wondering why I didn't try to go after my dreams. And I have to say, if I did kick the bucket right now? Sure, I'd be pissed that I didn't get there, but at least I have the satisfaction of knowing I was on my way."

Scott's heart constricted as he fought the urge to tell her that she'd made him think more, *feel* more, in the past few hours than he probably had in ten years. If ever. That, suddenly and inexplicably, the thought of never seeing her again bothered him far more than the possibility of not making it out alive.

But he didn't dare say that.

Not in words, at least.

"Christina?" he whispered, waiting for her face to lift to his before cupping her cheek. "This is nuts, but I want—" He swallowed.

"Go for it, Bucko," she whispered, then softly laughed, low in her throat. "Not like anybody's gonna know but us."

Or at least that's what he thought she said over his pounding heart as he lowered his mouth to hers.

Chapter Three

"Holy hell! Found 'em—!"

"They okay—?"

"Think so, although the gal looks like she's stuck. Frank! Hernando! Get your butts over here, *now!*"

Jerked awake, Scott batted at the bright light searing his eyes...until it registered that was the *sun* shining in his face.

"Hey, buddy—how're you doing?"

Scott shook the last remnants of sleep and disbelief from his brain as Christina stirred in his arms, then let out a little cry. Although whether from relief, surprise or pain, Scott couldn't tell.

"I'm fine, but she's—"

"Yeah, we can see that," the rescuer said, his voice graveled with both age and what had undoubtedly been a very long night. "It's okay, sweetheart, we're gonna get you outta there in two shakes." Then, to Scott, "You did good, keeping her warm like that. Can you walk?"

"Yes. At least," he said as he tried to stretch out his cold, stiff muscles, "I could before I fell asleep—"

"Good," the rescuer said as three or four other people appeared, bustling around Christina, "'Cause I need you outta the way so the paramedics can do their thing—"

"But—"

"Go check on your family," Christina said, her voice rough, "they must be worried sick." When he still hesitated, she shut her eyes and commanded, *"Go."*

"I'll be back. I swear," he said, although he doubted she'd heard him.

Stooped over, he crawled through the tunnel the rescuers had made in the destruction, releasing a nauseous gasp when he emerged into what looked like the set from a disaster movie.

Momentarily paralyzed, Scott struggled to absorb the scene as dozens of rescuers, some in National Guard uniforms, swarmed around him—the odd wall, still inexplicably standing; the sunlight dancing across the glass-littered ground, glancing off twisted pieces of what Scott realized in horror was a small plane; rows of seats, the leather furniture from the lounge upended, mutilated, half-buried underneath what had been the second floor. And above it all, framing the destruction, the blue, cloudless sky, serene and still and contrite, as though denying the fury it had unleashed only hours before.

"Scott! Thank God!"

He wheeled around to see Blake and Mike striding toward him, dusty and muddy and scratched up, but otherwise okay, and his head snapped back to the present. Then his cousin, Victoria, her dark curls a tangled, filthy mess, appeared, squealing as she threw her arms around each one's neck in turn, all of them talking at once.

"—ceiling caved in so we couldn't get out—"

"—Javier's in bad shape, they've already taken him to the hospital, Miguel's with him—"

"—Dad's in an ambulance, something about chest pains—"

"—Mom's got a broken wrist—"

"—but they had to give her something to calm her down," Victoria put in, tears brimming in her eyes. "Because, that flight attendant? She...she didn't make it." Scott swore as Mike laid a hand on Scott's arm, the uncharacteristic gesture raising the hairs on the back of Scott's neck. "They haven't found Emily yet, either."

For a moment, he couldn't speak. Couldn't think. Couldn't, for the first time in his life, make a decision. Try to find his sister or go back for Christina? Honor a promise he'd only made a few minutes ago, or his duty to family?

Frowning, Scott glanced back over his shoulder, then sighed. Meeting his brothers' gazes, he asked, "Where was Em when the storm hit?"

"Over there, talking to Aunt Virginia," Victoria said, pointing to where the lounge had been, then shuddering. "But then, so was I, and I ended up way the heck over there." Her arms folded across her ribs, she nodded toward the other side of the building, then started to cry. "Oh, God—what if Em's..."

She burst into sobs as Blake wrapped one arm around her shoulders, a moment before a shout went up from about twenty feet away.

"We got her!"

Scott and the others picked their way through the wreckage as fast as they could, getting to Emily right as the rescuers pulled her free. Like the rest of them, she was dirty and debris-ravaged, but, other than a wonky ankle, she seemed none the worse for wear.

Physically, at least. Because Scott wondered what sort

of psychological toll the last fifteen, sixteen hours would have on all of them, none of whom had ever been through anything even remotely life-threatening before. Certainly he would never be the same, he thought as he made his way back to where he and Christina had spent that long, cold, miserable night, only to find that she, too, was already gone.

"Where?" he asked a state trooper on the scene.

"Same place they took everybody else. San Antonio Memorial." The trooper looked over at his brothers and cousin. "Y'all need a ride?"

"I...I don't know." Forking a hand through his hair, Scott scanned the surreal landscape. "The cars—"

"All totaled," the trooper said gently. "Except for that Escalade over there. Some dings and scrapes, but otherwise intact. Probably drives okay. Strange, how these things happen. I've seen entire blocks wiped out, except for one house left standing, untouched." Away from the mangled building by now, the officer nodded toward the SUV, which did indeed look virtually unscathed. "A rental, I'm guessing from the license plate."

Scott nodded, his throat constricting. Around them, lights flashed, radios squawked from assorted emergency vehicles. Out of the corner of his eye, he caught Mike climbing into one of the ambulances, its siren bloop-blooping as it started away. "Yeah. Ours," he finally got out as he took in the crushed Explorer lying on its side.

"Then you'll be wanting these," the trooper said, digging in his pocket and handing over the keys. "They were in the ignition, so I figured I'd better take 'em. Not that I expect anybody to come out here looking for trouble, but you never know."

Scott nodded his thanks, then said, "My brothers, they

said…" His stomach turned. "Javier Mendoza? Do you have any idea where he is?"

The grave, compassionate expression in the man's gray eyes said far more than Scott wanted to hear. "That must be the guy they got to first, lying right past the doorway. He's probably already at the hospital by now, they can tell you more when you get there." The man rested a hand on Scott's shoulder. "You okay, son? That bruise on the side of your head bothering you any—?"

"I'm fine. Or will be, soon enough. Thank you."

The trooper's radio crackled; with a wave he walked away, the same moment a reedy, but surprisingly strong, voice called out.

"Oh, Scotty—thank God you're all right!"

Forcing a smile for his mother, Scott made his way through the angled vehicles toward her, the warm sun again giving the lie to the wicked, bizarre weather from the day before. Wrapped in a silver Mylar blanket and propped up on a gurney, her arm strapped to her chest, his mother accepted his kiss, then asked, with anxious eyes, if they'd found Emily.

"Yes. A few minutes ago—"

"Is she…is she all right?"

"She's fine. Her ankle's a little messed up, but you know our Em—can't keep a good girl down—"

"And Jordana?"

Figuring whatever they'd given her, combined with the trauma, was playing tricks with their mother's head, Scott said quietly, "Jordana didn't come, remember? She stayed at the resort—"

"No, no—she called me on my cell about ten minutes before the tornado hit, said she'd changed her mind and was getting a ride to the airport with that Tanner person." She

grasped Scott's wrist with her good hand, her eyes wide
with fear. "Oh, God, Scott—if she was on the road—"

"I'm sure she's fine, Mom," Scott said evenly, even if
his stomach didn't agree.

"All righty, Mrs. Fortune, we need to get going," the
attendant said, adding, as another pair of EMTs wheeled
Emily toward them, "Your daughter's going to ride with
you, how's that?"

"Emily, sweetheart…!"

As the last ambulance finally pulled away with his
mother and sister inside, Scott stood with his hands in his
pants pockets, a light, chilly breeze ruffling his hair as
he surveyed the decimated landscape—fences gone, trees
uprooted or snapped in two, entire windbreaks felled like
bowling pins. Oddly, the storm seemed to have inflicted far
less damage to the flight school building behind him—it
was still standing, at least—but Scott had overheard some
of the rescuers saying that this tornado was only one of a
series. That others—although not as devastating, thank-
fully—had also touched down in Red Rock itself, causing
even more damage.

Blake came up beside him, one hand on his hip, the
other cuffing the back of his neck. "Holy crap."

"That about sums it up."

"Think this is what's known as one of those life-altering
events."

A lot more than you know, Scott mused, his thoughts
drifting back to Christina—the heat of her hand gripping
his, her trusting weight against his chest…the lingering
buzz from that sweetly electric kiss. Still. Even in the clear
light of day.

Crazy.

But damn if he didn't feel as though somebody'd flipped

a switch in his brain…a switch he hadn't even known had been in the "off" position.

He looked back over Blake's shoulder to see their cousin picking through the debris, wobbling on her high-heeled boots like a tipsy mountain goat. "What on earth is Victoria doing?"

"Looking for her luggage, she said. I suppose it's giving her something to focus on so she won't freak out." Blake met Scott's gaze. "She keeps talking about some dude in a cowboy hat pulling her out of the rubble then disappearing. Got any clue who she's talking about?"

"None," Scott said, thinking he had far more pressing things on his mind than Victoria's mystery cowboy in shining armor. Like the woman who, in one night, had twisted him far more inside out than a tornado ever could. Not knowing how badly she was hurt…

Pulling the rental's keys from his pocket, Scott called to his cousin. "Vicki! We need to get to the hospital."

She looked up, shielding her eyes from the sun. The wind caught in her hair, whipping it around her smudged face. "But…my things…"

"Now, Victoria," Scott said sharply, walking to the SUV, his brother and muttering cousin following suit.

"Sorry," she mumbled after she got into the back. "I'm just hungry. And exhausted. And…" She let out a muffled sob. "And when I think—"

"It's okay, honey," Scott said as they slowly pulled away, the car's shocks working overtime as they drove over the chewed up ground. "We've all had a rough time."

And yet, he mused as they reached the highway, where it became much smoother going except for the occasional jagged branch or chunk of somebody's shed, not once during their ordeal had Christina complained. Even though she had to have been in pain. And frightened out of her wits.

If anything happened to her...

He stepped on the gas.

Not surprisingly, the E.R. was borderline chaos, all the exam rooms filled, a pair of obviously harried nurses doing triage on the dozens of walking wounded flooding the waiting room.

"Scott! Over here!"

Emily was in a far corner, between a resigned-looking older man pressing a bloodstained towel to a gash in his head and a mother with worried eyes holding a sleeping toddler. His sister's foot, wrapped in an ice pack, was elevated on a pillow on the glass table in front of her. Blake scanned the crowd. "Wow. Did San Antonio get hit, too?"

Emily shook her head, her pinched brow the only clue she'd been through hell. "No, just Red Rock. This is overflow from the Medical Center. Look," she said, nodding toward the TV mounted high on the opposite wall, where a camera panned parts of the town, showing the damage. Considering what might have been, though, things could have been much worse.

For all of them.

He turned back to his sister. "Where's Mom and Dad?"

"In treatment rooms. Mike's been toggling between the two of them. I'd bug the desk for more information, except, one, I can't exactly move and, two, I'm afraid of that nurse. Yeah, that one, in the pink scrubs. Don't let the teddy bears fool you—she's fierce." The man with the bleeding head was called to see the doctor. With a heavy sigh, Victoria plopped into his vacated seat, laid her head on Emily's shoulder. She smiled for her cousin, then said, "Eventually

I'll get into the inner sanctum and find out what's going on, but…"

She glanced across the room, then whispered, "It's Javier I'm most worried about, if the look on Miguel's face is anything to go by."

Scott twisted around to see Javier's and Marcos's brother, who'd come from New York for the wedding, sitting in a chair on the other side of the room, his head in his hands.

"Go on, talk to him," Blake said. "I'll check on Mom and Dad."

Looking far more bedraggled than the rest of them, Miguel shakily stood at Scott's approach. A small, tight smile strained his mouth. "Your family—is everybody okay?"

"More or less. Miguel—for God's sake, sit, you look like you're about to keel over. How is he?"

"It's bad, man," Miguel said, sinking onto the seat, strangling his still wet ball cap in his hands. "Real bad." Terrified brown eyes lifted to Scott's. "He's…he's unconscious, they don't even know yet what needs fixing. His head, his legs…" The young man swallowed hard, obviously fighting for control.

"Damn…" Scott felt as though someone had put a stake through his chest. "You need me to make any calls—?"

"No, I already talked to Marcos. He'll get in touch with everybody else." He looked at Scott, obviously fighting tears. "I found him, right after the twister hit. I could tell he was in bad shape, but there wasn't a damn thing I could do—couldn't call 911 because the cell service was down, couldn't go get help because the roads were trashed. Best I could do was keep the worst of the rain off him, but…" Shaking his head, he looked away, a tear tracking down his filthy, stubbled cheek.

"Hey…" Scott laid his hand on the younger man's shoulder. "It's going to be okay. He made it through the night. That's got to count for something—"

"I can't stop thinking," Miguel went on, his left leg bouncing, clearly not hearing any voices except the nasty ones in his own head, "what if he didn't get help in time—?"

"And you're only going to make yourself crazy, worrying like that," Scott said, even though his own voices, making him worry and wonder about Christina, weren't doing him any favors, either. When he spotted Blake, he waved him over. "I need to go check on my folks, but Blake will stay with you until your family arrives. And listen," he added as he stood, "you know we'll help in any way we can. Whatever Javier needs, it's his. Got that?"

Miguel looked up, hope and terror fighting for purchase in red-rimmed eyes. "Thanks."

"No problem."

Despite Emily's warning, Scott had no choice but to confront the obviously frazzled nurse at the desk. "Yes?" she snapped, not looking at him.

"I'd like to see my parents. Virginia Alice and John Michael Fortune?"

"Rooms 1B and 1A," she said, jabbing a pen over her shoulder, "right on the other side of the door—"

"And you have another patient who came in by ambulance around the same time, Christina Hastings? Can you tell me which room she's in?"

"She a relative, too?"

"No, but—"

"Only family's allowed to see the patients, sorry."

"You're not serious?"

She frowned up at him. "Do I look like I'm in the mood to kid around?"

Frankly, Scott guessed that was a mood she was never in. "Then can you at least tell me her condition?"

"No."

Scott leaned over the counter, close enough to make the woman back up. "If it hadn't been for my family," he said in a low voice, "it's highly unlikely Miss Hastings would even need to be here right now. So if you don't mind—"

"Do you see all these people, Mr. Fortune? Do you also see how many more of them there are than us? Now, please, go see your parents and let us get on with what we're supposed to be doing. Which includes taking care of Miss Hastings."

When the woman turned her back on him to answer another staff member's question, Scott realized he'd lost that round. Which did not sit well. But, he thought as he strode toward the exam rooms, damned if he'd lose the next one.

He heard Mike's agitated voice before he entered their father's cubicle. Sitting with his ankle crossed over his other knee, his brother was on his phone, conducting business as though his Gucci suit wasn't filthy and ripped, his thousand-dollar loafers caked in mud. More than that, however, as though their father wasn't dozing in a hospital bed six feet away, hooked up to an army of machines and looking more vulnerable—more human—than Scott had ever seen him.

Tearing his eyes from his father, he said to Mike, "Somebody's gonna be all over your ass about that cell phone. If I were you I'd switch to text."

Behind him John Michael snorted. "Took you long enough."

Okay, strike the *vulnerable* part of that description.

"Been a little busy, Dad." Scott glanced at his brother, getting to his feet and walking out of the cubicle, presumably to continue his conversation without interference. "And Mike's been with you."

Their father grunted, his eyes drifting back closed. "True," he said, his breathing slightly labored. "I can always count on Mike."

And some things never change, Scott thought, although frankly he was too worn out—and this was neither the time nor the place—to take umbrage. "How are you feeling?"

"I've been better. But it's nothing a good night's sleep and some decent food won't cure."

"So the pain in your chest—?"

His eyes opened again. "Gone. For the most part. It's nothing, don't know why everybody's making such a fuss. They want to keep me overnight. Can you imagine?"

"I think that's called doing their job."

John Michael pulled a face. "Sticking it to my insurance company, if you ask me. I intend to fly back tomorrow, though. You'll make the arrangements, won't you? Might as well fly out from San Antonio. No sense returning to Red Rock."

Scott crossed his arms. "Don't you think you should wait to hear what the doctors have to say?"

"Flight's only two and a half hours. If need be, I'll hire a nurse to go with us. Which reminds me, how's your mother?"

That he should ask about her as an afterthought was no surprise. That it should irritate Scott so much now, when it never had before, was. "I'm about to go look in on her now. Victoria said she was pretty shaken up—"

"No surprise, there. Virginia always has been emotionally fragile."

"Dad. She just spent the night trapped in a tornado-demolished building. I think she's entitled to be a little shaken up."

His father gave him an unreadable look, then said, "Go on, tell Virginia I said to get some rest, but we're going to be on a plane tomorrow. We need to get home, dammit. And send Mike in, I need to talk to him…"

Moments later his mother greeted him with a slightly dreamy, "Oh, hello, dear," when Scott walked into her room. Leaning against the side of her bed, Scott took her good hand.

"How are you doing?"

"Better, now." She frowned at the cast on her wrist, as if not sure how it got there, then yawned. "Although whatever they gave me for the pain makes me very sleepy. And apparently—" she yawned again "—I also got a nasty bump on the back of my head. There goes next week's hairdressing appointment," she said on a sigh, then crinkled her pale forehead at Scott. "The doctor said your father and I are going to be moved upstairs, that we should stay overnight. As a precaution."

"I think that's very wise. Don't you?"

"I suppose," his mother said on another puff of air. "Although I'd rather be home. In my own bed." Virginia Alice grimaced down at the hospital gown. "Wearing my own things…oh, dear!" Her gaze shot to Scott's. "Our luggage! Whatever happened to it?"

"I don't know, to be honest. Could be in the next county, for all I know."

"I see." She thought a moment, then said, "Well, then, I suppose someone will have to pick up something for me to wear on the trip home. Since I certainly can't be seen in public in this!"

Scott smiled. "Not to worry, Victoria and I will take care of it."

Her eyes lifted to his. "Do you suppose they have size twos in San Antonio?"

"If not, I'm sure we can find a box of safety pins some-where." When she pulled a face, Scott chuckled, then said, "And by the way, if Dad gets his way you'll be back in your own bed by tomorrow night."

Virginia smirked. "And since when has he ever not?" Then she sobered. "Any word from Jordana yet?"

"No." He squeezed his mother's hand. "Sorry."

She nodded, then pressed Scott's hand to her soft cheek. They'd gotten her cleaned up, but without makeup she looked even more frail. "Thank you for not spewing out some platitude, telling me not to worry. Worrying is what I do."

"No kidding," he said, and she softly laughed, then low-ered their hands.

"You know why I do, don't you? Because your father doesn't. Or won't let himself, in any case. So I have to do his worrying as well as my own." She shrugged. "'Tis my cross to bear."

Smiling, Scott leaned over and kissed her forehead, get-ting a faint whiff of her familiar perfume, as though after using it for so long it was permanently embedded in her skin. "Get some rest, and I'll check in again later. As he turned to leave, however, Virginia called him back.

"Your father and I…I know how our relationship must seem to you kids at times—"

"Mom, this isn't the time—"

"I watched a woman d-die in front of me, Scotty. I thought *we* were going to die. That has a way of making you…think about things. About what matters. And what matters to me, right now, is that you and your brothers and sisters understand that, for all the…stuff your father pulls, I love him. And I know he loves me. Yes, there are times I want to smack the man senseless, for taking me for granted, for making me feel I come in a distant second to the business…"

She struggled to sit up straighter. "But I knew who he was when I agreed to marry him. Just like he knew I was a tenderhearted fool who jumped at the sight of her own shadow," she said with a smile. "I also see a side of him he refuses to show to you kids, for whatever reason. Yes, your father's the most stubborn human being on God's earth, but deep down, he's a good man who's always only wanted the best for his children. And don't you ever forget it."

Virginia sagged back against the pillows, her eyes fluttering. For a long moment Scott simply stood there, stunned, until her breathing slowed into a deep, easy rhythm—she was asleep.

Nurse Ratchet was still at her post at the nurse's station, sparing Scott the merest glance as she handed off a folder to another nurse.

"Your parents are being moved upstairs in about a half hour—"

"Not why I'm here."

She sighed. "Still can't tell you about Miss Hastings—hospital policy."

But before "Screw hospital policy" could leave Scott's lips, another nurse strode past, calling out, "Dr. Karofsky says to call County General, tell 'em we've got an orthopedic transfer."

"Name?" she barked to the other nurse as she snatched up the phone.

"Hastings. Christina."

Scott lunged across the counter to grab the phone out of her hand.

"Mr. Fortune! Don't make me call security, now—"

He waggled the phone. "I'd like to see you try," he said, and she huffed out a breath. "Why are you transferring her?" His gut twisted. "Is she...does she need some kind of special care?"

"No! She's—" Apparently realizing she'd stumbled right into his trap, the nurse sighed heavily. And held out her hand for the phone, which Scott relinquished. "She's fine. Broken foot, some bumps and scrapes, that's it. But she's uninsured. And we're a private hospital. Although we'll treat anybody who comes through that door, once they're stabilized we transfer them to a public facility. She'll be well taken care of there, I assure you—"

"She'll be taken care of right here," Scott said, yanking his wallet out of his pants pocket and throwing down his American Express card. "Consider her bills paid."

With a *Mama told me there'd be days like this* eyeroll, the nurse picked up the card, slammed it back onto the counter lip. "Then go settle it with Admitting. Right on the other side of those doors."

"Thank you." He snatched his card and stormed back to the E.R. lobby, barely stating his case to the gal behind the glass when he heard a shrieked, "Scott!" behind him. He spun around to see a breathless, disheveled Jordana rush across the lobby, an equally disheveled Tanner Redmond right on her heels, Jordana's luggage in his hands.

"Jordy! Thank God!" Scott said, all the air punched out of his lungs when Jordana threw herself into his arms, then launched immediately into a disjointed narrative about her changing her mind at the last minute and Tanner giving her a ride, except the car ended up in a ditch when he swerved to avoid flying debris, something about a shed, and the weather, that the National Guard guys who'd helped them pull the car out of the ditch had been at the airport and knew the family was here.

"Is everyone okay?" she now asked, shoving a hank of loose, stringy hair behind her ear. She was flushed and dirty and a mess and, strangely, the look suited her. An appraisal he'd keep to himself.

He quickly filled her in, then pushed out a breath. "Javier, though…"

She sucked in a breath. "He's not…?"

"He's alive, but unconscious. According to Miguel, it doesn't look good."

"Oh, Scotty, no…" Jordana's eyes filled with tears. "Is his family here yet?"

"On their way, I gather. And Mom's been worried sick about *you*."

"Oh, Lord, I can imagine. I'd better go see her…well—" Smiling, she turned to Tanner, her hand extended. "Thank you…so much. For everything."

Setting down the larger bag, Tanner frowned. "Um… you're welcome. You sure you don't need me to stick around?"

"No, really," she said, relieving him of her carry-on and grabbing the roller case's handle, jerking it up. "I'm fine. But thanks. Again."

A second later she and her luggage were gone. Scott turned to Tanner, standing with his hands in his pockets, his expression pensive but otherwise unreadable. "Thanks for looking out for my sister," Scott said. "Appreciate it."

Green eyes glanced off his. "No problem," Tanner muttered, then turned and stalked back out the door.

"Sir?" the woman behind the glass called. "I'm ready to finish up here if you are."

"Yes, of course," Scott said, returning to the window, hardly able to believe all his family obligations—for the moment, at least—were taken care of and he could finally attend to the one item on his never-ending checklist that didn't feel like an obligation at all.

In fact, what he felt as the admissions lady buzzed him

back inside the E.R., was something that felt an awful lot like…anticipation.

What a rush.

Chapter Four

Her foot splinted and Ace-bandaged within an inch of its life, Christina frowned at the nurse bustling around her. "What do you mean, you're getting me ready to go up to orthopedics? I thought I was being transferred?"

"Change of plans," she said with a bright grin.

"I don't understand, I can't afford…" She blinked back hot tears. It wasn't being poor that bothered her, it was having to tell people she was. "I know what the deal is, that y'all are only supposed to make sure I'm not bleeding to death or anything—"

"Your bill is being seen to," said the thin, pretty doctor with a Russian accent as she entered the tiny room. "So you can stay right here, all right? And you will be good as new in no time."

"Define *no time*," Christina said, even as she tried to make sense of the first part of that message. Someone was paying her bill?

Hugging her clipboard to her flat chest, the doctor shrugged. "The breaks are not bad, so a few weeks, perhaps." When Christina groaned, Dr. Karofsky smiled. "And maybe you will be a good candidate for a walking cast. You should count your blessings," she said, her brown eyes softening. "The paramedics told me how they found you. We were worried, that your injuries would be much worse."

"I know, I'm very lucky—"

"Although you might not think so tomorrow. You still took quite the beating—you are probably going to be very sore…ah." At the sight of someone coming through the door, the doctor turned, smiling. "And here is your prince, I think." She jerked her head sideways to the nurse, and they both left, leaving Christina alone with Scott.

She flushed so hard and fast she felt like she was having heatstroke, as the memories came flooding back, about how he'd kept her talking, kept her from losing it, which naturally led to remembering The Kiss…which if she had a grain of sense she'd never think of again. Except there he was. Standing there. In the full light of day.

Yeah, good luck with that, babycakes.

"How are you—?"

"How's your family doing—?"

"They're all okay, for the most part," Scott said, yanking a metal chair around and straddling it backwards, the familiar, almost intimate position—like they were old buddies simply yakking in her kitchen—oddly unsettling. Especially since actually seeing him again only emphasized how waaaaay out of her league he was. And not only because he was a pretty boy, but his whole…bearing, the grace and ease with which he moved, how he managed to look almost regal even all messed up…

Then he smiled. A full-out, *You have no idea how glad I*

am to see you smile that started in his eyes and kept going. She half expected to hear angels sing.

"And you?" he said, still grinning like a fool, at which point it occurred to her she looked like something nasty the dog dragged in. Maybe the trauma had affected his eyesight.

"A couple of the bones in my left foot are broken," she finally got out, casually lifting a hand to tuck some of the hair that had worked out of the braid behind her ears, "and I'm banged up some. But otherwise, I guess I'm okay. Relatively."

"Do you need me to call anybody about looking in on Gumbo?"

Her heart knocked in her chest. "No…I mean, thanks, but I had one of the techs call my landlady, so it's all taken care of."

"Then he's okay?"

Christina nodded, momentarily unable to speak. "He's fine. Enid—she's my landlady—said a tree fell over, made a big mess in front of the office, some shingles got ripped off, but that was about it." Her brow puckered. "You remembered my dog's name?"

Now the smile went a little crooked. This was not going well. "You only mentioned it, oh, a dozen times or so. It stuck."

"Sorry, I guess I'm a little…attached."

"It's okay, I know the feeling."

"You have a dog, too?"

"Had. A horse. When I was a kid. His name was Blackie."

Christina snorted. "Original."

"Cut me some slack, I was only eight. And anyway he had some fancy-ass registered name I could never remember. Man, I loved that horse."

"You rode?"

"All of us took lessons, but I was the only one who stuck with it. When I left for college, though, Blackie went to live with a family with a little girl. I still miss him. Miss riding." A shadow seemed to flicker across his face before he smiled for Christina again, which made his eyes go all crinkly in the corners. God help her. "Gumbo's lucky to have you. How old is he?"

"Not real sure. He was still a pup, though, when he showed up out of nowhere one night, about five years ago. We were having this terrible storm, and suddenly through all the thunder and thrashing outside I realized there was a dog whining and scratching at my door…so I opened it and he ran right inside like he'd been waiting on me to let him in. Shook water all over me," she said with a little laugh, then sighed. "Funny thing, he happened into my life right when I needed…"

Realizing she was about to say *Someone to love me,* Christina jerked herself back to the here and now. "Is it true? That you're picking up my tab?"

His eyes latched on to hers and would not let go. "Yes."

"You didn't have to do that."

"Apparently I did, according to their rules."

"County General's okay—"

"I'm sure it is, but it's also damn inconvenient."

Christina frowned. "For who?"

"Me. Since it's hard enough to keep an eye on everybody without your being in another hospital."

Flushing again, she looked down at her lap. "Why do you think you have to keep an eye on me?"

When he hesitated, she lifted her eyes to his again, seeing in them a weird mix of confusion and determination. "I don't have to. I want to."

Apprehension pricked her skin. "Scott—"

"And you do not want to pull some pride number on me, okay? The only reason you were in that airport yesterday was because we were flying out of it."

"So you feel...responsible?" Her brow knotted again. "For something you couldn't possibly have foretold, let alone controlled?"

Their gazes locked again and she forgot to breathe. "For the tornado?" he said. "Of course not. For you?" His gaze softened. "Absolutely."

Oh, dear.

His cell phone buzzed in his pocket at the same time a tech appeared from behind the curtain with a wheelchair.

"All righty," the jovial guy said as Scott got to his feet, "time for your field trip upstairs."

"Then can I go home?"

"That, I couldn't tell you—"

"Javier's family is here," Scott said, "I need to go see them—"

Now settled in the wheelchair, Christina looked up. "Javier?"

Another shadow settled in Scott's eyes, this one far darker, and more ominous, than before. "The guy who drove some of us to the airport. My sister's brother-in-law, nicest guy you'd ever meet. He's...he's in critical condition."

"Oh, Scott..." Christina wrapped her hand around his. Words were useless, she knew. But sometimes it helped simply to know somebody cared. "I'm so sorry. Really."

Scott looked down at their joined hands, gave hers a gentle squeeze, then left.

"You part of the family, too?" the tech asked as he wheeled Christina out to the elevators.

"Not hardly. You might say fate…blew us in each other's path."

The tech chuckled. "You ask me, dude doesn't look like he's exactly unhappy about that."

So not what she wanted to hear.

Nearly as many Mendozas filled the waiting room as had been at the wedding, although obviously the mood was much more somber this time. Scott recognized Luis, Javier's father, and Javier's next youngest brother Rafe, an attorney who'd recently opened an office in Red Rock, as well as a slew of more distant relatives whose names he didn't remember. Wendy threaded her way over, shooting him a *Don't say it* look.

"Marcos is worried sick. There's no way I'm not going to be here with him. I saw the others—they went down to the cafeteria to get something to eat." Wendy glanced back over her shoulder at her father-in-law, who was sitting very still with his hands clamped to the armrests, listening to Rafe, before she led Scott a little further away. "The E.R. doctor said they've taken Javier into surgery."

"For…?"

"His legs. His head. To relieve the swelling. The doctor…he suggested the family contact their priest. Just in case." Her eyes filled. "The head wound…they're not giving any guarantees."

Muttering a curse, Scott patted Wendy's arm, then returned to the family. Javier's father stood and gave Scott a wan smile, although he looked ten years older and much grayer than he had barely a week before.

"We're very close friends with a top-notch neurologist in Atlanta," Scott said quietly. "He's the best in his field. I'm sure as a favor to the family he'd be more than willing to fly in for a consultation—"

"Thank you, son," Luis said, "but we wouldn't want to put you to any trouble—"

"It's no trouble, I assure you." He glanced at Wendy who'd come up beside him, her hand in her husband's, then back at Luis and his two other sons. "Besides, we're all family now, right?"

Smiling sadly, Luis touched Scott's arm. "You're very kind. But if you don't mind, I'd like to see what the doctors here say first."

"Of course."

At a staff member's suggestion, the family then headed off to the surgical unit's waiting room. A moment later the ambulatory Fortunes returned from the cafeteria, Emily hobbling along on crutches.

"Here," Blake said, handing Scott a white paper bag smelling of burgers and fries.

"Not hungry. But thanks."

"Take the damn food. And eat it. Or you're going to pass out. Speaking of which, we got a couple of hotel rooms nearby. The girls desperately want to get cleaned up, and honestly we're all about to collapse. Mom and Dad are both asleep, there's not much else we can do here. Mike and I had another couple of rental cars delivered so we don't have to travel in a pack—"

"You all go on ahead. I can't leave yet."

"Scott." At the sharp tone to Blake's voice, Scott frowned at his brother. "The world will manage without you long enough to catch a shower. And eat. And buy some clean clothes." He smirked. "Even you can deal with jeans and a T-shirt for a day."

Scott had to admit his brother was right—while everything was in limbo no one would miss him for an hour or so. So, burger and fries in hand, he forced himself to walk out of the E.R. doors and across the parking lot to the Escalade...where he wolfed down his food so fast he barely remembered eating it.

But instead of following the others to their hotel, or stopping to pick up clothes that didn't smell like a swamp, he drove back to the airport. Why, he wasn't sure. To convince himself it hadn't all been a bad dream? To come to terms with what had happened? Maybe.

But as he drove the fifteen miles or so along a gently rolling road that stretched out to forever, underneath a clear blue sky that stretched even farther than that, he realized what he had to come to terms with was whoever he was now. Because, for good or ill, he sure wasn't the same person he'd been a week ago.

Twenty-four hours ago.

He'd ignored *What-the-hell?* twinges, confusing and crazy, that had plagued him for the past few days—the bizarre whisperings that *this* was home. The more they'd persisted, the more firmly he'd shoved them into that dank, musty storeroom where he kept all the other *maybes* and *somedays* and *when the time is rights*.

Until a rogue tornado came along and ripped that storeroom all to hell and back, dumping all those *somedays* right smack in his face.

And with them, a pretty little gal whose raspy, wispy voice belied her steel core, whose determination to make her own somedays actually happen had shaken Scott far more than the storm.

Hell, up to that point he could have sworn he didn't even believe in love, let alone love at first sight. And yet...

And yet.

Feeling like a car commercial stunt driver as the SUV navigated the choppy terrain, Scott noticed Tanner's Jeep parked in front of the flight school building, then the man himself, walking the perimeter with his hands in his back pockets, scanning the damage. Which was more extensive than Scott had at first realized. In fact, in the almost surrealistic stillness the whole scene reminded him of a war zone photograph.

At Scott's approach, the other man offered him a nod and a grim smile befitting the bleak picture, the brim of his ball cap shadowing his eyes. "What're you doing here?" he asked mildly.

"Not sure. I think I simply needed...to see."

Tanner looked away. "I heard Sherri didn't make it."

"The flight attendant?" Tanner nodded. "Did you know her well?"

"Not really, no. I mean, we crossed paths maybe a couple times a month. Still. It's hard to take in, you know?"

"Yeah."

Tanner toed a small pile of crumbled, waterlogged masonry. Overhead a buzzard circled, hopeful and eerily graceful, like something out of a bad horror film. "How's your...family?"

"Doing okay. Dad's determined to leave tomorrow."

That got a short, dry laugh. "Yeah, your father struck me as the kind of man who wouldn't let a little thing like a tornado disrupt his plans. No wonder Jordana—" He stopped, shaking his head.

"What?"

"Nothing. By the way, I spotted some luggage in the ruins."

"You're kidding?"

"Nope. Figured you might want it. Couple of carry-ons, one larger bag. They're in my car. Would've brought it back to the hospital, but now you've saved me the trouble. Might be more," he said, leading Scott back to where he was parked, "but that's what I could get to." He helped Scott tote the bags back to the rental, then stuck out his hand to firmly shake Scott's.

"Y'all have a safe trip," he said, then strode back to his own vehicle, and Scott took a deep breath, a breath full of clean, sweet Texas country air, and simply...let go, giving in to something far more powerful than his own will.

Or even, he thought with a wry smile as he climbed back behind the wheel, his father's.

It always surprised Christina, on the rare occasions when she saw her mother, how disconnected they were. Like they weren't related at all. And frankly she wasn't even sure why she'd called Sandra, told her what had happened. She was even less sure why her mother'd come. Especially since Sandra had made it more than plain from the moment she walked into Christina's room that not only was her boss at the restaurant where she worked as a hostess, a job she'd held on to, according to her, "for security," even after her remarriage—not happy about her leaving early, but that she couldn't stay because she needed to get back to Houston ASAP. Probably to fix Helpless Harry—Sandra's husband, although not Christina's stepfather by any stretch of the imagination—his supper.

"But...I could use some help getting home," Christina said. "Since you're here and all."

"Oh." Sandra checked her watch. Something flashy. Christina was guessing Harry had Money. Taste, no. Money, yes. Then blue eyes rimmed with far too much eyeliner met Christina's. Her mother had been pretty, once upon a time, blond and cute and curvy. And she still was, on a good day, in the right light. Hospital fluorescents, however, were not kind to older women with penchants for fake tans and frosted lipstick. Her all-black outfit wasn't helping, either. "But…if I hadn't come, what would you have done?"

After Christina's father walked out—there'd been some talk of Christina's being a "surprise," that her father had only married Sandra out of guilt—Sandra hadn't exactly embraced single motherhood with grace and fortitude. Oh, she'd done her best, Christina never doubted that. Unfortunately, her "best" hadn't been very good.

"Never mind," Christina said, even though she had no earthly clue what to do. She didn't have cab fare, if she could even find a driver willing to haul her all the way to Red Rock. And her seventy-eight-year-old landlady didn't drive anymore. At least not that Christina knew about. She supposed she could call Jimmy, her boss, for a ride, but the very thought made her skin crawl. Recently divorced, Jimmy was a lonely man. A fact which he took great pains to impress upon Christina every chance he got.

"Oh, now, I'm sure you'll figure out something," her mother said. "You always do. Here," she said, upending a used Walmart bag onto the end of Christina's bed. Out tumbled a pair of blindingly purple Spandex capris and a badly pilled, black and silver sweater, along with a pair of underpants—at least three sizes too large—and a stretched-out camisole top. "I brought you some clothes, like you asked. But I didn't figure there was any point in bringing one of my bras—it would be way too big for you. Don't bother returning them, it's all stuff from the Goodwill pile, anyway."

Christina stared at the clothes, closer to tears now than when she'd thought she might die. Which at the moment seemed preferable to wearing these clothes. She never asked, or expected, anything from her mother, but just this once—since, you know, she *had* cheated death and all—would it have killed the woman to drop a few bucks for a pair of Hanes sweats or something? Some new underwear in Christina's size—?

"Oh, good—you're still here! They said at the nurses' station you were being discharged."

She looked up to see a grinning—and cleaned-up, she noticed—Scott, precariously hanging onto a potted plant, a ridiculously large stuffed hound dog, a box of candy and a helium-bloated "Get Well!" balloon in about a thousand eye-popping colors, bobbing up near the ceiling.

And her heart stuttered.

"And who is this?" her mother asked, her nostrils flaring like a bloodhound catching a scent.

"Mama, this is Scott Fortune. He…he and his family were also in the airport when the tornado hit. Scott, this is my mother, Sandra."

Somehow he shifted all the offerings into his left arm to shake her mother's hand. "Do you live in Red Rock?"

"Oh, good Lord, no. Not anymore. Been in Houston for several years now." Then her eyes narrowed. "Fortune? Related to the Red Rock Fortunes?"

"Distantly, yes." Scott set the plant on Christina's rolling food tray, handed her the dog. "I'm from the Atlanta branch of the family."

"I see," Sandra said, her voice frosting, and Christina's face warmed. Especially when her mother shot her an all-too-familiar look. "So your family will be returning to Atlanta, I suppose?"

"Tomorrow, if all goes well," he said, and Christina breathed a sigh of relief, that he was leaving, taking her inappropriate feelings with her. Because the last thing she needed was some rich dude who kissed like he invented it and brought her stuffed hound dogs. And dumb balloons.

"Well, honey," her mother said, "you take care of yourself," and vanished, leaving Christina wondering exactly who else she thought was going to.

Witnessing the obvious lack of affection between Christina and her mother, Scott realized he'd take his mother's obsessive worrying about her children any day. At least she *cared*.

But if her mother's aloofness—she hadn't even kissed her daughter goodbye, he realized—hurt Christina, she didn't let on. That is, until she gave Scott a bright smile that was so fake it made his chest ache. "What's this all about?"

"I couldn't decide what you'd like."

Blushing, she cuddled the stuffed dog to her hospital-gowned chest, her gaze fixed on the top of its head as she fingered the soft plush. "You know, you're not obligated to bring me presents just because...we, um, kissed."

The barest hint of melancholy in her voice turned him inside out. As though people didn't give her gifts very often. Or kissed her.

"Actually," Scott said as he eased himself onto the edge of her bed, "if I think a woman's worth kissing, I think she's worth at least flowers. Or a box of candy."

"Or a stuffed animal?"

"She has to be *really* special to warrant one of those."

Suddenly, she met his gaze, mischief tangoing with the wistfulness in her blue, blue eyes. A very strange, and oddly appealing, combination. "The kiss was that good?"

"*Amazing* is the word that comes to mind."

"Oh, stop," she said on a cute little giggle. Then she set the dog aside, patting it as if saying goodbye. "You're very sweet. But you didn't have to get me anything at all. Let alone half the gift shop. Also—" she sighed "—I have no idea how I'm gonna get all this stuff home."

"Then I guess I'll have to take you."

Her eyes shot to his. "I can't let you do that. You've got your family to think about—"

"All under control," he said, adding when she opened her mouth to protest, "Really. My parents are quite safe here for the night, and the others have hotel rooms. Strange as it might sound, nobody needs me."

Christina stared at her lap for what seemed like forever, then picked up the box of chocolates, slipping one finger underneath a seam in the cellophane and carefully peeling it away. "I wish I could say I don't, either. Need you, I mean." The box open, she carefully selected a piece of candy, popped it into her mouth, then held the box out to Scott, who declined. "Oh, right. You don't like sweets." She shrugged. "More for me, then."

Genuinely bewildered, Scott folded his arms. "I don't understand."

"About why I wish I didn't need you? I don't expect you to. So…I'm simply going to say thank you for the gifts— I'm crazy about chocolate, as you can probably tell—and for offering to take me home. Since I hadn't figured out how I was going to get there. Although…" Her forehead creased. "Fair warning—my place…it's nothing special."

"And why on earth would I care about that?"

"Because, well…we're not exactly talking Ethan Allen here."

Remembering his Atlanta decorator's horrified expression when he'd proudly shown her the Ethan Allen sofa he'd picked out all by himself for his condo's living room, Scott smiled. To Christina, Ethan Allen clearly had a different connotation than to dear Aileen, to whom Ethan Allen reeked of *bourgeois*. Poor woman never had recovered.

"I'm sure it's fine. But couldn't your mother have taken you?"

"Apparently not. And now I need you to leave so I can get dressed." She grimaced at the strange assortment of clothes piled on the bed, picking up the shiny, lurid purple…things. "Although *dressed* might be overstating it."

Chuckling, Scott left her to it. But he'd no sooner shut her door behind him than his phone buzzed—a text from Wendy: In OR waiting room. Dr here. Where r u?

On my way, he texted back.

Twenty minutes later, Scott stood on the hospital's rooftop deck, his phone clamped to his ear. He'd caught Dr. Rhodes as the man was about to leave for the very gala the Fortunes were supposed to be hosting. Scott succinctly relayed what Javier's surgeon had said about his case—that they'd operated to relieve the pressure, were keeping him in a medically induced coma until the swelling subsided— then released a sigh.

"They're not even being 'cautiously optimistic.'"

"Understandable, given the circumstances. Although obviously I can't comment, not being familiar with the case—"

"That's why I'm calling. To see if you'd consider flying out—on our dime, of course—to see Javier yourself."

"Damn, Scott…I'm sorry. With my schedule that would be very tricky. But you said San Antonio Memorial?"

"Yes."

"Liz Cuthbert's head of neurology there, as I recall. We did our residency together a million years ago. She's excellent, trust me. In fact, if I ever needed a neurologist, I'd want it to be Liz. I swear. Look…what I can do is give her a call, make sure she's aware of the case. And I'll be glad to consult by phone, if Liz thinks it's warranted. But your friend is in very good hands already. And their rehabilitation facilities are second to none."

"If you're sure…"

"Couldn't be more so. Can't promise miracles—I learned a long time ago that way lies madness—but I can promise you if any team could pull him through, it's that one. But, from the sounds of it, you all are damn lucky things weren't a lot worse. Please give my best to your parents, won't you?"

Marginally reassured, Scott slipped his phone back inside his pocket and returned downstairs to check on his parents. His mother was overjoyed to be reunited with her luggage, especially her carry-on with her jewelry.

"Jewelry can be replaced, Mom," Scott said, as she pawed through the various pieces with her good hand, her eyes alight.

"And if I'd bought it for myself, I'd completely agree with you. But your father gave me each and every one of these. And that can't be replaced. And yes, I know he probably had his PA pick out half the pieces—"

Try all of them. But whatever.

"—but in his case, it really is the thought that counts. Especially since I know he's never bought jewelry, personally or otherwise, for any other woman. Except for your sisters, of course," she added with a smile.

That much was true, at least, although his mother's conviction was a testament to her faith in her husband. That, or the services of a private investigator. Still, for all his father's faults—his workaholic tendencies, his emotional detachment—he'd never cheated on his wife. And not, Scott knew, for lack of opportunity, since he'd witnessed first-hand his father rebuff any number of all-too-eager, would-be successors to his mother. And with, as far as Scott could tell, not even a trace of regret.

Oh, yeah, his father had left broken hearts strewn all over Atlanta. But his mother's was not one of them.

As if on cue, John Michael appeared at the doorway to his wife's room, the only man on earth who could manage to still look dignified in a faded hospital gown and wrinkled cotton robe. "I asked the nurse to bring my meal in here so we could eat together," he said, and his mother beamed.

"What a good idea!" She giggled, her loose hair around her face making her look like a girl again. "I ordered the fish. How about you?"

"The same." With a heavy breath, he took the chair beside her bed, his mouth curving at the sight of the jewelry. "Got you that bracelet when Emily was born, as I recall."

"You did indeed," his mother said, her "told you" gaze sliding to Scott's.

Perhaps it wasn't as difficult as he'd thought to understand what bound them to each other. After all, there was a lot to be said for simply knowing the other person would never leave you.

Which he supposed began, he mused as he left his mother's room and started the long trek back downstairs where—he hoped—Christina was waiting, with finding someone you never wanted to leave.

Chapter Five

By the time Scott returned, Christina had had some time to think over a few things, not the least of which was to wonder what on earth had prompted her to apologize for where she lived. It was what it was, she was who she was, and since he was leaving the next day, anyway, what the heck difference did it make?

"Turn left at the light, then keep on to the end of the road."

Scott glanced over at her, his brow drawn. "How're you doing?"

"Just dandy." She glared at the lovely, knee-high contraption she was sporting, courtesy of the House of Frankenstein. Which hadn't seemed so bad while she was still in the hospital. Out here in the wild, however, especially when she factored in the crutches...

"If it's any consolation," Scott said, "I broke my foot my senior year of high school." A grin pushed at the corners of his mouth. "And please don't ask how. My brothers still won't let me live it down. But anyway, I had the boot, the crutches, the whole nine yards. In my case, for eight weeks." He sighed. "So much for that track season."

"You ran?"

"Not that year, I didn't. I did, however, make straight As. Since there wasn't a whole lot else I could do other than study. And play Nintendo. Although I have to admit…" The grin spread. "There were certain…advantages."

"Ah. As in, pretty girls falling all over themselves for the privilege of lugging your backpack around?"

"More than could be numbered."

Christina sputtered a laugh, only to feel her eyes sting. Because in her case there would be no entourage eager to fetch and carry and wait on her. Oh, her landlady would certainly help out, but Enid had her own life, and there was only so much she could do. All her old friends had either moved or married and had their hands full with husbands and houses and little kids…

The stinging spread to the back of her throat, forming a lump. How on earth was she going to manage, with no car, no job, this blankety-blank cast…?

When a renegade tear slid down her cheek, Christina dug in her purse—which one of the rescuers had amazingly found in the rubble nearby—for a tissue to blow her nose, hoping Scott wouldn't notice.

"Hey," he said, and she thought, *So much for that.*

"What?"

"It's going to be okay."

"Sure."

"I mean it—"

"You have no idea what I'm facing, Scott," she said, his equanimity suddenly irritating the very life out of her. "None. And since you don't, you have no right to tell me everything's going to be okay. You don't know that. *I* don't know that. So please—spare me the platitudes."

Silence stretched between them until he said, "I take it reality just hit?"

She snorted. "Like a ton of bricks. Sorry."

"No apology necessary. Nice to see you're human, after all. But…you don't think I'd understand what you're going through?"

"Not a whole lot, no."

"Because…?"

"Because that hospital bill you took care of without a blink? Would've taken me years to pay off—"

"Which is maybe why I paid it?"

"And I'm grateful, I really am. But it only points out how different we are. That you're so used to things coming easy for you there's no way you could even begin to comprehend what life is like for the rest of us peasants. Now you've done your good deed you can tuck yourself into your thousand-count Egyptian sheets at night with a clear conscience…what are you doing?"

Gravel sprayed as he yanked the car off to the side of the road by somebody's pasture. In the distance, by a stand of trees, a half-dozen fat and sassy horses grazed. The engine cut, Scott twisted to face her, his left hand gripping the steering wheel, the anger in his eyes boring straight through her.

"Hopefully setting you straight." His gaze darkened. "I work hard for my money, Christina. I've earned it. As has my whole family. And I'm not going to apologize for it, or them, or pretend this isn't who I am because it offends you." When she turned away, her face hot, he said, "I know you're scared, Christina—"

"I'm not—"

"Don't even give me that. Right now you're like a

wounded animal backed into a corner, lashing out at me not because I have money, but because you're afraid I'm somehow going to make things worse. Not that I blame you. You don't know me from Adam, for one thing. And, for another, no matter what I say you're going to think I'm patronizing you. Which irritates me no end, but I get it. *However,*" he said when her eyes cut back to his, "I didn't pay your bill, or offer you a lift, so I could check them off some hypothetical 'good deeds' list."

Christina broke free of that penetrating gaze to look out the windshield. "Then why—?"

"Because I *like* you, dammit. Is that so hard to believe?"

"Why?" she said again, more softly.

"I don't know, maybe because you're *likable?*" he said, adding, when her eyes bugged out of her head, "But the why is immaterial. The point is, there's no way I'm leaving you in the lurch. You're going to need help, honey. And I'm going to make sure you get it. Because that's how I roll."

After a brief but intense conscience-grappling session—although why she should feel guilty about accepting whatever assistance he could give, she had no idea—Christina blew out a long, shaky sigh. "You must think I'm a few sandwiches short of a picnic."

"No," Scott said with a sigh as he pulled back onto the highway. "I've dated crazy before. Trust me, you don't even come close. But I do wish you'd judge me by what I do. Not what I am. That you'd simply…give me a shot."

She could feel her heart beat throbbing at the base of her throat. "At…what?"

"Well, to begin with…how about the chance to prove I'm a human being and not a stereotype?"

"Oh, Lord…" Christina lifted one hand to her flaming face. "I deserved that, didn't I?"

"'Fraid so, petunia," he said with a light laugh, then glanced over. "So do we have a deal?"

"Sure," she said, since, at the moment, it didn't appear she had much choice. Although whether Scott was her guardian angel, or she'd just made a pact with the devil, remained to be seen.

She was an odd little duck, that was sure. His entire adult life Scott never been able to tell if women were interested in him or his bank account—a major reason why he'd never let himself fall in love, most likely. Christina, on the other hand, almost seemed afraid of his money. Or, at the very least, found it suspect.

Go figure.

"It's right up there—you can't miss it."

Gravel from the disintegrating blacktop crunched under the wheels as he pulled into the parking lot. "You live in a motel?" he said, regretting the question the instant it left his mouth.

"*Used* to be a motel," Christina said. Almost cheerfully, as though maybe that air-clearing a few miles back had done some good. One could hope. "Since, as you may have noticed, this is no longer a through road, about twenty years ago Enid—that's my landlady—and her husband Eddie converted it to apartments. After a fashion."

Scott's gaze swung to the murky, leprous hole in the ground in front of the units. "I take it the pool is no longer in service."

"Not since I've been here. I'm up at the far end, by the way. No extra charge for the second window."

"Good deal."

"I thought so."

He parked in front of her unit. The architecture was strictly midcentury Minimalist—varicosed stucco walls, plain brown numbered doors, slider windows, a flat roof. A five-foot overhang sheltered the cement slab "porch," dotted with a couple of banged-up molded plastic chairs, a kid's lower-rider tricycle, a cheap charcoal grill.

A scene that by rights should have been unrelentingly dismal. Except for the occasional wind chime or sparkly porch ornament, a glittery Christmas garland entwining one of the porch posts, a wreath of bright red poinsettias on one door. And, lining the entire edge of Christina's allotment of porch real estate, pot after pot of multicolored pansies, bravely shivering in the cool breeze.

"Home is what you make it, you know," she said, as if seeing the picture through his eyes.

"I couldn't agree more."

He got out to help her from the car, saw her bite her lip as she fitted the crutches under her arms. "Lean on your hands."

"That hurts, too."

"I know. But this will hurt less. Trust me."

"Say that enough times," she grumbled, hobbling to her door, "I might eventually believe you."

After several obviously frustrating moments trying to juggle her purse, her keys and the crutches, Scott took the keys to unlock her door—behind which he heard very excited whining and scratching.

"Should I be worried?" Scott asked as the lock tumbled.

"Only if you're in the way."

He pushed the door open, barely avoiding the four-legged torpedo that shot out, a bow-legged, stout-bodied, floppy-eared canine concoction whose sole purpose was to love, love, love. Laughing, Christina practically threw down the crutches to somehow lower herself to the porch, where she wrapped her arms around the wriggling mass of unbridled bliss, burying her face in his golden brown ruff.

Scott sternly told himself it was stupid to be jealous of a dog. Okay, maybe not jealous. Envious?

Still dumb.

"Hey, guy—gotta pee?" A question that apparently ratcheted up the excitement factor another level or two, before, with a joyful woof, the pooch bounded like a jack-rabbit for the stand of trees a few feet away and did his thing.

"Tough little dude," Scott observed.

"Yup. Like a gymnast. Lots of power in a small package."

Gumbo sauntered back, grinning like he was hot stuff, the tail wagging the entire dog. Then he seemed to notice Scott, schlurping his tongue into his mouth and cocking his head, his furry forehead furrowed before he sidled back to Christina. Scott could have sworn the dog nodded in Scott's direction as if to say, *So who's the dude?*

Still on her rump on the porch, Christina lifted her eyes to Scott. "Sorry. I don't bring…visitors here very often—"

"Ohmigosh, you're back!"

Scott no sooner hauled Christina to her feet than a scrawny redhead in a flowered housecoat, a bright orange down vest and a pair of scuffed-up sneaker clogs grabbed Christina out of Scott's grasp and into her own. For a moment he feared for Christina's rib cage. The woman barely came up to Christina's chin and had arms like a plucked chicken, but that was one fierce hug. Then she let go, her painted claws clamped around Christina's elbows as she scrutinized her from head to broken foot. "Lord, child, where did you get those clothes?"

"My mother. 'Nuff said. Scott, this is my landlady, Enid Jackson. Enid, this is Scott Fortune. Scott and I…got trapped together in the same part of the airport. After the tornado."

From behind a pair of burgundy glasses that had been cutting-edge ten years ago, Enid's beady gray eyes latched on to his like a burr to a dog's underbelly.

"Fortune? As in the family that owns half the ranchland in these parts?"

"Distant cousins. But yes."

Arms crossed underneath where her bosom should have been, the old woman studied him for what seemed like an eternity, then gave a sharp nod. "Thank you for bringing my girl home. I would've come to get her myself, but my sight ain't what it used to be. In fact…" Her carefully drawn eyebrows plunged as her gaze swung to Christina. "I don't suppose you're gonna be doing much driving for the next little while."

"No," Christina said on a sigh. "And not only because of my foot. Ellie Mae…they told me she didn't make it."

When Enid softly groaned and again took Christina into her arms, Scott wondered if the storm had claimed another victim he wasn't aware of, until Enid said, "She was a good old car. I'll miss her."

"Yeah. Me, too. Now if you don't mind…I need to get inside and put my foot up."

Not waiting for an invitation, Scott simply gathered Christina's things from the car and carted them in behind her. Enid had gone ahead and was helping her settle onto the plain beige sofa at right angles to a slightly lopsided taupe recliner, the once-plush fabric worn shiny on the arms. The room looked pretty much as he'd expected, the few pieces of furniture dull and threadbare, cheap fake pine paneling smothering the walls, the appliances in the bare-bones kitchenette chipped and scarred and sorry.

You deserve so much better than this, he thought, appalled in spite of himself. And humbled, as he realized how much greater her struggle to leave even the tiniest scratch on the world, let alone a mark, was than his had ever been. No wonder she resented his life and its relative ease. Yes, he worked hard, not only to support his very comfortable lifestyle but also to overcome the trust fund baby stigma. For damn sure he wasn't a slacker. Still, Christina was right—he'd never, not once in his entire life, worried about money.

Or had to live like this.

And yet...the banged-up appliances gleamed, he noticed. Bright prints obliterated much of the tacky paneling. A cheerful patchwork quilt gently hugged the back of the bland sofa. On a stubby little table, a small fake Christmas tree proudly shimmered in a patch of late-afternoon sunlight pouring through the window. The *spotless* window. And against one wall, cinder block-and-board shelving bowed under the weight of hundreds of books.

What Christina lacked in means, he realized, she more than made up for in spirit. And that spirit, her spirit, permeated the small space with something the best decorator in the world couldn't supply, easing inside him as importunately as Gumbo—now wedged on the sofa beside his mistress—nudged at Christina's hand until, laughing, she scratched his head.

Questioning blue eyes lifted to his, a slight smile curving her lips. Behind her, Enid fussed over something in the kitchenette. "You don't have to stay, you know. And your family must be wondering what happened to you."

"I suppose I should check in on them. Especially since they're all leaving in the morning."

Her hand stilled in the dog's fur. "They? Aren't you going with them?"

"No. I—" He stopped, having no idea what to say. How to explain something he didn't yet fully understand himself. "Will you be all right for a while?"

"You're coming back?"

"Soon as I take care of a few things, yes." He met Enid's very astute gaze. "Can you keep an eye on her for a couple of hours?"

"You bet. Especially since I'm guessing our girl's about to pass out, anyway."

"Just go on and talk about me like I'm not here," Christina said, yawning and tugging the quilt off the sofa's back, snuggling underneath it with her dog.

He glanced back when he reached the door. She was already asleep, Gumbo's head protectively propped on her thigh, the dog's big brown eyes clearly saying *Mess with her and you're dead meat. Got it?*

Yeah. He got it.

John Michael glowered at Scott from the high-backed upholstered chair in his hospital room. "Don't be ridiculous. Of course you're coming back with us."

His arms folded across his chest, Scott stared his father down. "No, I'm not. Someone needs to stay to keep tabs on what's going on with Javier, for one thing—"

"You can keep tabs every bit as easily from Atlanta."

"This isn't a business deal, Dad. This is Wendy's brother-in-law. Family." Wendy, who at the staff's insistence had gone home to rest, had updated him on the phone shortly after Scott left Christina's. Javier had come through both the orthopedic and neurological procedures as well as could be expected, but now the wait-and-see part of things began. "The family's so stressed…if I can help in any way, I'd like to."

His father pushed out a heavy breath. "But your work—"

"Nothing Mike can't handle for a few days."

John Michael's heavy brows lifted. "So *now* you're sharing? And don't give me that look. You two have been like two dogs fighting over the same bone since you were babies."

"I didn't think you realized—"

"The competition between you?" His father barked out a short laugh. "Who do you think fostered that rivalry? And why wouldn't I? It made both of you work harder, didn't it?"

Not that Scott hadn't suspected as much for years. Still, hearing it voiced... "In other words, you sacrificed your own sons' relationship for the business."

"Oh, don't be so damn melodramatic. The family, the business...it's all the same thing." His father lifted his hands, the fingers tightly linked. "All *one* thing." His hands dropped back into his lap, then he sighed. "I suppose you're right, though. About staying around for Javier. For Wendy's sake. No need to upset her any more than she already is. Now what was the second thing?"

"The second thing?"

"You said *for one thing*—meaning Javier—from which I deduced there's another reason you want to stay. So what is it?"

He hadn't planned on telling his father about Christina—especially not before he had it sorted out in his own head—but there was nothing to be gained from not being honest. To a point.

"The young woman I was trapped with—Christina. Her foot's broken, meaning she's going to be laid up for some time. I don't feel...it's right to leave before I make sure she's taken care of."

His father frowned. "She doesn't have family? Friends?"

"Her support system is apparently pretty meager. Nor can she afford nursing care."

"And she knows you're a Fortune."

"Well, yes, obviously she does. Although she hasn't

asked for anything, I assure you," he said to his father's *Watch out* frown. "But the least we can do is make sure she's okay. And since I'm hanging around for Javier, anyway…"

"One week, Scott," his father said, jabbing his index finger in Scott's direction. "You make sure this…Christina has whatever she needs, then you get your butt back where it belongs. Is that clear?"

"Perfectly," Scott said, knowing, as he left his father's room, that he wasn't going to feel any differently in a week than he did right now…that there was something here he needed. Something he'd risk everything he'd ever known, ever been, to get.

He doubted his father would ever understand. But for the first time in his life, Scott thought as he climbed behind the steering wheel, right now he didn't much care.

At the purr of Scott's rental car pulling up in front of her apartment, Gumbo bounded off Christina's lap and boing-boinged across the floor to the front door to sniff and whine and wag until Scott let himself in. Two days, two years, whatever, it made no difference to a dog—they were now friends for life.

"Hey, guy—no, this isn't for you, so back off." Gumbo now in retreat—for the moment—Scott grinned over at Christina, holding his prize aloft, and her heart boing-boinged worse than the dog. Which was getting to be a habit. A very, very bad one.

"How're you feeling?"

"Better," she lied. The doctor had been dead-on about how sore she'd be. Her foot didn't even hurt that much anymore, but man, every muscle in her body ached. Since she didn't want to get too cozy with the big-gun pain meds, however, she'd been popping Tylenol like there was no tomorrow. Not that it helped much.

"Have you been moving, as the doctor suggested?"

She glared at Scott. "You bet. What's in the bag?"

"Dinner. From Red. Some new chicken dish Enrique came up with. You hungry?" he said, heading into the tiny kitchen for plates and flatware while holding a nonstop, one-sided conversation with the dog. This person who'd been waiting on her hand and foot since his family's return to Atlanta was definitely not the same uptight dude who'd flinched at the idea of drinking plain coffee…a metamorphosis she'd been observing with a combination of amusement and sheer terror.

Because let's be real here, boys and girls—she could like this new, improved Scott Fortune a whole lot. Yes, even more than she'd liked the old one. Not good. Especially since she figured he probably saw her as some sort of, well, charity project.

"Sure," she said, even though she rarely felt like eating much, what with her only exercise these days being getting up to pee every few hours or point the remote. Whoopee.

Humming, he carted in their food, setting hers on the TV tray that had become a permanent fixture beside the sofa, and the light from the lamp played across his handsome face, provoking all sorts of prickles of a sexual nature. Which only went to prove that God did indeed have a very strange sense of humor.

"I hate this," she muttered.

Scott frowned. "You haven't even tasted it yet."

"No, I mean *this*." She waved her hand toward her foot, stretched out in front of her underneath one of her long summer skirts, which were easier to deal with than jeans. "I'm not incapacitated, I can walk with the crutches—"

"After a fashion. And you also know if you don't keep the foot elevated it will take longer to heal."

"Are you always this irritatingly logical?"

"Yes. Are you always this argumentative?"

"Only around irritatingly logical people," she grumbled, hefting her fork to begin her nightly ordeal of picking at her food. Except when she finally put a bite into her mouth, she practically swooned. "Ohmigosh, this is good."

"Told ya," Scott said, his crisp, upscale khakis, deep blue dress shirt and la-di-da sweater—part of the haul overnighted from various online clothing companies to replace his lost luggage—so at odds with the poor old recliner it almost hurt to look at him. Them. "I called a medical supply company, by the way. Said they'd have a shower chair delivered in the next couple of days."

"I'll make sure I'm here, then," she said drily, only to then notice half her food was already gone. Wow.

"So," Scott said, looking all relaxed and whatnot in the chair. As opposed to Gumbo, who was about to quiver his fur right off at the prospect of something, anything, falling off Scott's plate and into his mouth. "You up for taking down the tree tonight?"

Christina's gaze swerved to her little tree, still valiantly twinkling away in the corner. "Or I could simply let it stay up until next year, save the trouble of doing it all over again."

"I did that one year. When I was, I don't know…eight or nine, maybe? We were all allowed to have a tree in our rooms, if we wanted. And that year I decided to decorate mine with action figures. GI Joes and He-Man stuff, mostly. Coolest tree ever," he said, chewing. "Couldn't bear to take it down. So I didn't."

"Ever?"

"Might still be there, for all I know," he said, and she laughed. Then she sighed.

"It is tempting, to leave it up. But if I do, what've I got to look forward to next year?"

Setting his plate on the floor—to Gumbo's unbridled joy—Scott propped his elbow on the arm of the chair to rest the side of his face in his hand. "You really see yourself in the same place next year? In your life, I mean?"

His question caught her up short. "I...don't know. I hadn't thought about it."

"Then maybe you should," he said softly, rising to take her plate, as well as his dog-slimed one, to the kitchen.

"No," she said to his back, making him turn. "No, you're right...of course I don't see myself in the same place."

His smile warmed her heart. And scared the heck out of her. Nobody ever paid this much attention to her, ever. Or cared two hoots about her plans. Her dreams. To be treated like a grown-up, and an intelligent one at that...

"Good girl," he said, then pointed to the tree, one eyebrow raised.

Christina nodded, sighing as Scott began to dismantle it, handling the cheap ornaments like they were precious heirlooms.

Just like he's handling you, she thought, stifling a sudden urge to throw something at the man.

Scott had meant what he'd said—to his father, about feeling a responsibility to help Christina; to Christina, about genuinely liking her. Nor could he deny the immediate *whoosh* of attraction, off-the-wall though that had been. However, if he were being honest, another thought had niggled, that those feelings would pass. That the mist of infatuation would clear and he'd see Christina as simply a sweet, very pretty young woman who could use a help-ing hand. Period.

Four days on, he was pretty sure he could put that worry to rest.

Especially since he'd seen Christina at her worst, during those four days—frustrated and cranky and given to peri-odic bouts of pure muleheadedness just for the heck of it, as far as he could tell. Once or twice she'd even snarled at him. But was he put off?

Nope.

And how could he be, when she'd also laugh at herself for being such a pain in the butt. Or compliment his cook-ing skills, such as they were, with a sparkle in her eyes that turned him inside out. Or ask him what courses he thought she should take to help her reach her goals. And with every laugh, every tease, every sparkle, the mist cleared a little more, leaving Scott even more convinced that while adren-aline and testosterone might have fueled that initial, kick-to-the-head reaction, neither accounted for what he was feeling now.

What the next step was, however, was anybody's guess.

He'd spent most of the day putting out metaphorical fires Mike couldn't, or didn't want to, handle back in At-lanta. Now he pulled up in front of Christina's apartment, making a mental note to research an outfit that could fix that pool. Enid's insurance would take care of the tornado damage, but he was guessing the pool had fallen victim to insufficient cash flow. That, he could handle...

He saw Christina's curtains twitch as he got out of the car, a bouquet of flowers in hand. A moment later the land-lady came out onto the porch, silently shutting the door behind her and huddling inside a heavy cardigan against the night's chill. They'd only chatted a couple of times since Scott brought Christina home, but now the old woman's protective, suspicious expression, even in the jaundiced light from the caged bulb over the door, put him on alert.

"I'm just leaving, I think my hanging around was making her twitchy," Enid said with an eyeroll behind the glasses. "But she's already had supper, dog's been fed, too."

"Thank you—"

"So what's your deal with her, anyway?"

"Pardon?"

The old woman snagged his arm—with a far stronger grip than he'd expected—and tugged him out into the parking lot, where she crossed her arms over her bony chest and somehow managed to back him against his own car.

"Mr. Fortune, not that I'm not appreciative of everything you've done for Chrissie, but you need to know…that gal's been through the mill. Been screwed over too many times by too many people. That she's as sweet as she is, is nothing short of a damn miracle. So you feel sorry for her, or what?"

"As in, pity her? No. Do I think she deserves better than life's given her so far? Absolutely." He palmed the car's fender. "I take it you don't have a problem with that?"

"Depends."

Scott suppressed a grin. Barely. A lesser man—or a smarter one, perhaps—would be halfway to the hills by now. "Mrs. Jackson—I promise you I only want to help. And I can give her whatever she needs—"

"Oh, I imagine you can *buy* her plenty. But before you go bandying around the word *give,* you might want to think about what that really means."

Okay, that gave him pause. Because…did he? Know how to give in the way she meant it?

"Are you saying she's fragile?"

"Oh, hell, no. Gal's as tough as they come. She's had to be, you know? That don't mean she might not mistake your…kindness for something more. That she can't still be hurt. That she's not still hurting. And I'm not talking about her foot."

"I didn't think you were—"

"I love that little gal like she's my own, and that's the Lord's truth. More'n her own mama ever has, from everything I can tell. So the last thing I want is for some fancy man to come along and break her heart all over again. Do I make myself clear?"

"Perfectly. Are we done here?"

"No." Enid backed up, barely, her eyes pinched nearly closed. "I ain't never been rich, Mr. Fortune. But I cleaned houses for enough wealthy families over the years to come to a conclusion or two about 'em. Either they pretend the poor don't exist, or they're curious about us, like we're a different species. Christina don't need you being *fascinated* with her, that's all I'm saying."

Scott pulled in a deep, steadying breath through his nose. Even though her sentiments weren't far off from the very thoughts he'd been wrestling with, they still rankled. "Mrs. Jackson," he said quietly, "my mother drilled it into all our heads from the time we were babies that people are people, that who they are isn't defined by what they have. Or don't have. I'll admit, I am fascinated, because I've never known anyone like her. But when I say that, I'm talking about her character. Who she is. Not *what* she is. Do I make *my* point clear?"

Several seconds passed before a soft cackle fell from Enid's shapeless, wrinkled mouth. "I guess you do at that. Don't mean I'm still not keeping my eye on you."

And he thought the dog was bad. "Wouldn't have it any other way," he said with a little salute, then walked back to Christina's door, realizing he'd been gripping the flowers hard enough to practically bend the stems.

* * *

Over Gumbo's excited barking, Christina yelled, "Door's open, come on in! Dog! For crying out loud, hush!"

Scott's entrance sent Gumbo into his happy-happy-joy-joy dance, his long tail wagging so hard it was a wonder it stayed on.

"Sit," Scott commanded, and after some effort the poor animal managed to lower his wriggling butt so it hovered right above the carpet, eyes glued to Scott in rapturous adoration. To complete the look, one ear, then the other, slowly flopped out.

"That's as close as it gets," Christina said fondly. "Something about the way he's put together, he can't get his backside all the way to the ground."

Then she noticed Scott had turned his frown on her and a chill snaked through her whole body, and that was the sorry truth. Good Lord, he was big. Bigger than she remembered, frankly. Or maybe it was only that her apartment seemed smaller.

"Why're you looking at me like that?"

"Like what?" he said. Still frowning.

She sighed. "Like your little chat with Enid isn't sitting so well." The dog looked from Scott to her, figured nobody was paying attention to him—which would never do—so he sashayed over to the sofa and hopped up beside her. Wedging his sturdy little body between her hip and the cushioned back, he laid his head on her lap with a contented groan. "Those flowers for me or the dog?"

"You can share," he said, handing her the bouquet. "You heard us?"

"Your voices, yes. Not what y'all were saying." She buried her nose in the delicate lavender mums, the scent fresh and sweet, then lifted them to Scott again. "I don't even own a real vase, but you might find a jar under the sink that'll work. I take it she was doing her Rottweiler number on you?" she said as he crossed to the kitchen.

"I was thinking more along the lines of rabid Chihuahua, but yes."

"She means well," she said over the water's thrashing into a big olive jar. "And it is nice to have somebody on my side."

Scott returned with the flowers, which he set on the fabric-covered footlocker she used as a coffee table. Still standing, he pushed back his jacket, shoved his hands in his pockets. Frowned some more. "I'm on your side."

"I mean somebody who's gonna stick around."

Silence. Then: "She wanted to know what my intentions were. Toward you."

"Oh, for heaven's sake," Christina said, even as she thought, *Yeah, wouldn't mind knowing the answer to that one myself.* "She sure has the wrong end of the stick there, doesn't she? I mean, you've been real sweet and all, but—"

"But what I haven't been, is entirely honest."

"About?"

Chafing his palms together, Scott sank onto the edge of the old recliner, pushed out a short, dry laugh, then lifted his eyes to hers. "Okay...those hours we spent together in the airport...jarred something loose in my brain. *You* jarred something loose, and...I don't want to say too much, too soon—the last thing I want to do is scare you off—"

Like she had any place to go?

"—and anyway, at first I thought...well, never mind what I first thought, that's immaterial now. Because the thing is, the more time we spend together, my feelings—for you, I mean—they're becoming more...real."

Then he gave her That Look. Like the one the Jane Austen hero always gives the heroine when he finally comes to his senses.

Except that's always at the end *of the movie, you goober! Not the frickin' beginning!*

"Scott," she said when she finally found her voice. "You can't be serious. Besides the fact we met less than a week ago...I'm not even remotely your type!"

A half smile tilting his lips, he leaned back, his hands gripping the chair's arms. Nice, strong hands, she couldn't help but notice. Because she was observant like that. "Yeah, well...I've dated plenty of women who were supposedly 'my type' and have never felt...drawn to them the way I am to you."

Christina opened her mouth to argue, only to hear a little voice in her head *pssst* at her, reminding her there was no arguing with Scott Fortune. Men like that, once they made up their mind, that was it.

Except...what was it he'd made his mind up about, exactly? So he was "drawn" to her. Big whoop. Didn't mean anything would come of it. Especially since...

"May I remind you, in case it escaped your notice, that my home is here? And yours isn't?"

"Well aware of that—"

"And even if that weren't the case, I simply do not have the wherewithal right now to be in a relationship. Or even think about one. So if there's an ulterior motive behind your wanting to help out, you might want to rethink a thing or two."

He laced his hands high on his stomach, looking completely relaxed. And not the least bit perturbed. Except the steely look in his eyes sent another one of those shivers scooting up her spine.

"So Enid was right. That you've been screwed over?"

Christina's eyes narrowed. "What did she tell you?"

"Nothing more than that."

"Then let me fill in a blank or two. I was married before,

when I was very young. It ended badly. I've dated some since then, and those relationships all ended badly, too—"

"Which is why you haven't dated in two years?"

"Did kinda put me off, yeah," she said, wondering what else she'd said that night that he'd remember. And she might not. Ergh. "And I finally realized," she said, hoisting her little booty back on track, "I needed to stop trying to define myself by looking to other people. Especially the wrong people. Because until I figure out who I am, I have no earthly idea who I need. Or what I need."

He tented his fingers in front of his face. "And why do I get the feeling you're leaving out several huge chunks of the story?"

"Because it's kind of hard to break free of the past if you keep revisiting it."

"None of us can fully escape our pasts, Christina—like it or not, the past shapes who we are—"

"Not if we don't let it. The sores are healed over. For the most part, anyway. Please don't ask me to rip them open again."

They stared each other down for some moments before Scott said, "I don't give up easily."

"Then this should be interesting, because I don't give in easily. Not anymore. And I told you, my home is here."

Seconds ticked by, punctuated by another groan from Gumbo.

"You're absolutely sure of that?" Scott said at last.

"Yep. So, see?" She lifted her hands, palms up. "Pointless."

"Okay, then," Scott said, getting to his feet and heading to the door, "I'll…see you tomorrow."

Except, after he left Christina didn't feel all that relieved, truth be told.

And that made her very, very nervous.

Chapter Six

"Here," Wendy said, setting a towel-covered basket on the wrought-iron table in front of him, along with a knife and butter dish. "I made muffins."

Glancing up from his iPad, Scott smiled for his sister, her dark brown hair glowing in the morning sunlight flooding the whitewashed, glassed-in porch snuggled up against the back of her and Marcos's modest three-bedroom house in town, where he'd been bunking since the family's return to Atlanta. Apparently, the former leather-and-chrome "décor" had been centered around the big-screen TV in the living room, until she'd wrought her magic. Now Barebones Bachelor Pad was turning into a fun, funky mix of contemporary sleek and cozy cottage, as sassy and sophisticated as its new mistress.

"You spoil me," Scott said, setting down his coffee mug to pluck a still-warm pumpkin muffin from the basket. "And aren't you supposed to be off your feet?"

Air rushed from Wendy's lungs as she sat across from him, then dragged over another cushioned chair to prop up her feet, a pair of puffballs underneath her fuzzy slipper socks. It was pretty obvious she was about to go stark raving bonkers from boredom. And, Scott suspected, loneliness. After finally convincing Miguel it was okay for him to return to New York, Marcos was rarely around, between tending to his duties at Red and frequent trips to San Antonio with his father and Rafe to keep tabs on Javier. In which case, considering the shenanigans his sister *could* get up to, a baking binge was the least of their worries, her puffy ankles notwithstanding.

"Giving you breakfast is hardly spoiling you," she said. "Especially since this is the first morning I've caught you before you left again. I mean, I know you didn't hang around to keep *me* company, but still." She faked a pout, only to immediately grin. Then she grabbed her own muffin, yanking it apart like a starving urchin and slathering it with soft butter. "By rights, I should be mad at you."

Scott frowned. "For what?"

"Usurping my position as the family's black sheep."

"Nobody ever thought of you as a black sheep. A lost one, maybe," he said with a smile. "But not black."

Chewing, his sister waved one hand. "Whatever. But my point is, I was always the one voted most likely to do something crazy. Not you." She reached for the rest of her muffin. "You do know they all think you're nuts, right?"

Thinking, *Oh, just wait,* Scott leaned back in his chair, his gaze wandering outside and past their yard, to the vast, serene sky delicately veined with bare tree branches...as his thoughts wandered to that conversation with Christina, where she'd declared she'd never, ever leave Red Rock.

"They can think what they like. For the first time in my life, I feel as though things are finally making sense."

"Poor baby. You've really got it bad, don't you?" When Scott nodded, she laughed. "So you're telling me Christina is as down with...whatever this is as you are? After a week?"

"I didn't say that," he said, which got a snort from his sister. Scott glowered at her, then looked outside again. "As you said. It's only been a week. Right now I'm just in...the exploratory stage. Not anywhere near ready to sign on the dotted line."

Which was never going to happen as long as Christina kept him at arm's length, doling out bits and pieces of herself as though they were rationed. True, he might have given the impression that if she didn't want to talk about her past, that was her prerogative. And in theory he was fine with that. Except it bugged the life out of him, that she didn't trust him. Not entirely, at least. Understandable, he supposed, given the circumstances, but—

"May I say something?" When Scott faced his sister, a crease marred the otherwise smooth space between her brows. "I know you're used to making things go your way. Heck, we all are. Especially after hearing our entire lives how anything's possible if you work hard enough for it." A wry grin twisted her mouth. "Or throw enough money at it. But—and bear in mind I don't know Christina, so I could be talking through my hat—" The crease deepened. "This is a human being we're talking about. Not a business transaction. Have you considered how you're going to feel if she never...comes around?"

"What makes you think she won't?"

"What makes you so sure she will?"

Inexplicably annoyed, Scott got to his feet, grabbing his

leather jacket off the back of his chair and digging in the pocket for the keys to the SUV.

"And now I've chased you off," Wendy said, clearly amused.

"Brat," Scott muttered without heat, and she chuckled. "By the way, have you talked to Blake since they left?"

Although still several years older than Wendy, his youngest brother and baby sister shared a special bond that had been cute as all get-out to witness when they were little. And he knew they talked nearly every day, even now. "No. Why?"

"He seems…I don't know. Different, somehow. I can't put my finger on it. So I was wondering if he'd said anything to you."

Scott shook his head. "No. Things were so crazy after the tornado I didn't really get a chance to talk to any of them. But…"

"What?"

"That experience…I doubt any of us are the same. Except for Mike," he said with a humorless laugh. "Nothing affects him. And I mean nothing. I swear, sometimes I think the man's an android."

Wendy laughed. "That would explain a lot. Oh…take the rest of the muffins to Christina, will you? Otherwise, I'll eat the whole batch. And that would be wrong."

He returned to get the basket, then met his sister's gaze, realizing with a rush how much he adored her. How much he'd like—

"Wanna meet her?"

A huge smile lit up Wendy's beautiful face. "Yes, please!" Then, on an "Oh!" she clapped her hands together. "She could help me pick out stuff for MaryAnne's nursery! Oh, don't give me that look—she's probably going as stir-crazy as I am, with her broken foot and all. And what woman doesn't like to help decorate? It'll be fun, I promise."

At the hope twinkling in his sister's eyes, he sighed. "I'll give her the message."

Leaning painfully on her crutches as Scott drove up, Christina stood on the porch watching Gumbo zigzag around the small plot of grass bordering the trees next to the complex.

"What are you doing outside?" Scott asked as he got out of the car. Completely at ease, like they'd never had that conversation. Brother.

She angled her head, squinting at him through the sun. Wondering when he was going to snap out of…whatever this was. "Drying my hair. Letting my dog do his business." Then, with a sigh, she looked back at Gumbo, sniffing in the weeds. Happy as a dumb clam. "Cleaning up after him is a bit tricky, though. Enid said she didn't mind if I let it go for a bit, it being winter and all, but I do."

Scott set the basket he was carrying—like he was Red Riding Hood or something—on the lopsided metal table by the front door, where Christina had dumped the scooper and stuff. Which he then grabbed. "I can do that—"

"Oh, no…I cannot let you clean up my dog's poop!"

"After mucking out a horse's stall? No contest."

And off he went to tend to a chore she guessed was not part of his usual routine, chatting away to the dog trotting alongside him, presumably to show him the ropes. Or whatever. Then Scott calmly disposed of the little package in the Dumpster at the end of the parking lot, looking ridiculously pleased with himself.

"Now that I'm completely mortified…" Christina mumbled as she thumped through the door. Scott washed his hands at the kitchen sink—thoroughly, she noticed—then disappeared back outside. For good, if he was smart.

But no. Because no sooner had she resumed her usual spot on the end of the sofa, her foot stretched out in front of her, than he and the dog returned with the basket. Which, no matter how he held it, made him look extremely silly.

"You really mucked out horse stalls?"

"I really did. I gather from your wet hair the chair finally arrived?"

"It did."

"So how was it?"

"The chair? Hard."

"I meant your shower."

"Awkward. But after a week of sponge baths? Glorious."

"Did your foot hurt? Without the cast, I mean?"

"A little. But I was real careful not to put any weight on it."

"Maybe you should have held off until I was here to help you."

Silence hummed between them.

"Wendy sent muffins," he said, carting the basket to the small kitchen table, then rattling around in her cupboards for plates and utensils and things. If not his dignity. "Pumpkin orange. Although she looks nearly as miserable as you do. She can't go in to work, Marcos is rarely around, and her doctor's told her to keep her feet up as much as possible until the baby comes. She's not taking it well."

The dog hopped back up beside her to stretch out on his back, paws in the air, head upside down in her lap. Like he was waiting for her to feed him grapes. "Tell her I feel her pain." Realizing Scott was watching her, she glanced up with a too-bright smile. "Bless her heart. Thank you," she said when Scott set a muffin and a glass of orange juice on the coffee table within her reach, then sat on the chair across from her. "Are we pretending everything's fine between us?"

"I wasn't aware things weren't."

"But you—"

"I know. And I apologize for spooking you. Eat your muffin. You won't regret it."

Realizing he'd given her an out, Christina picked up the muffin, pinched off a piece and popped it into her mouth, where it exploded into awesome. Except thinking about Wendy led to her asking how Javier was doing, and Scott's quiet, "No change," stirred up all the weird, unsettled feelings that had plagued her off and on for the past couple of days—even before that bizarre conversation—and killing her appetite.

When she set down the muffin, Scott reached over and touched her knee. She couldn't decide whether she wanted to smack his hand or grab it. "Hey. What's wrong—"

"I think about how scared everybody must be for him, and about that poor flight attendant..." Who he'd finally told her about a couple days before. "And here I sit, having the gall to feel sorry for myself because I'm laid up for a few weeks. It kinda puts things in perspective, doesn't it?"

He gave her a strange look. "I suppose it does."

Picking up the muffin again, she took a bite, fed a piece to the dog. "Still. It's driving me bats, that I have to let people wait on me. Do stuff I'm supposed to be doing for myself. It feels all...backwards." She sighed. "Not to mention dangerous."

"Dangerous?"

"Yeah. Because..."

"Because you don't like being waited on."

"No, I don't. I'm used to being the one doing the caring. Like with Enid. Or babysitting the neighbors' kids some-

times. That makes me feel good. This makes me feel...
weird."

"And would you feel the same way if, say, it was Enid
waiting on you? Or your mother?"

"Oh, honey—if it was my mother waiting on me I'd feel
like I'd been warped to an alternate universe. This was the
woman who'd leave the box of cereal and a cup of juice
where I could reach it so she wouldn't have to get up to
make me breakfast. When I was *three*."

"That's harsh."

"Whatever. It toughened me up."

"I don't think three-year-olds are supposed to be tough,"
he said gently, his eyes all sympathetic and whatnot, and
feelings she never, ever indulged tried to do a number on
her head. So she changed the subject.

"Do you have flashbacks? About what happened?"

That got another strange, pensive look, one that sent heat
racing up her neck. *Oh, for pity's sake, it was just a kiss.
Snap out of it!*

Never mind that was the first kiss she'd had in...a long
time. Hence the hot neck. Among other things.

"No," he finally said. "Actually, it all feels pretty much
like a dream."

Doesn't it just? she thought, then said, "It felt like that
for me then, too," she said, shifting to get comfortable. Like
that was even possible. "So I didn't realize it would come
back to haunt me like this later. I think I was a lot more
afraid than I realized." She smirked. "Or wanted to admit."

"You know what your problem is?"

Yeah. You.

"I'm borderline psychotic?"

"I'll take that into consideration. But I was thinking
more along the lines that you need to get out of here."

"Now that's just mean."

"I'm serious." He got to his feet, a man with a plan. Eyes all lit up and everything. "Where would you like to go?"

"Anywhere but this house," she said, then shut her eyes and released a breath. "And there I go sounding bitchy again—"

"Honey, believe me. You've got many, many miles to go before you reach bitchy."

"Not as many miles as you might think," she muttered, then directed a baleful glance at her foot. "But this thing…"

"You can ride in the back of the SUV with your foot on the seat, how's that? And I'll play chauffeur—"

Terror streaked through her. That he was being too nice, that she'd get too attached, that he *would* snap out of it and/ or leave…and then where would she be? "Scott, seriously, you don't have to do this—"

"Yes, I do. Now can you make it on your own or do you want me to carry you?"

She actually had to think about that for a second. Until reason returned, bless its little heart, and she said, "I'll walk. But can Gumbo come?"

Still on his back, the dog lifted his head to give Scott what Christina knew was the Starving Orphan face. "If he wants to, sure. So where do you want to go?"

"Not shoe shopping, obviously. But…how about the airport."

"Really?"

She nodded. "Gotta face the demons sometime, right? Besides, my car's still there. Or what's left of it. I need to say goodbye."

With Gumbo as his copilot, Scott navigated the meandering country highway as it sliced through miles of winter brown pasture, then Red Rock proper, before stretching out again on the other side of town and toward the airport.

Since his arrival, he'd driven this road maybe a couple dozen times at the outside, but it had already become as comfortably familiar as his ten-year-old leather jacket.

As had the chatty blonde in his back seat, he thought with a grin as she prattled on about how it felt like *months* since she'd been farther than her front porch.

"Oh, my…I knew I'd missed the open space, but I had no idea how *much* I missed it."

"I can understand that."

She paused. "I doubt it, Mr. City Boy."

He glanced at her in the rearview mirror, then refocused on the road while he was still able to tear his gaze away from her bemused grin. The impish gleam in those sky blue eyes. Ten points to him, for getting her out of that damn apartment. "It's true. Although I fought it tooth and nail that first week I was here. But now…" He paused. "Where other people might see nothing and nowhere, I see…possibilities. Freedom."

That apparently shut her up. If for only a second.

"We might make an honorary Texan out of you yet—oh, no," she said, twisting to look behind her.

"What?"

"There used to be the neatest old barn right in front of that stand of trees," she said on a sigh. "Judging from the chewed-up look of the land, I'm guessing the tornado got it. It hadn't been used in years, but it was like some sweet old man you get used to seeing every day." Another breath left her lungs. "That's so sad. That it's gone forever, never to be replaced."

The old barn, maybe not. But every couple of miles, it seemed, they passed a cleanup or building crew, like beavers in hard hats, setting things to rights. Because, by and large, human beings were an optimistic lot. Or at least Texans were, Scott thought with another smile.

When they passed the spa where Scott and his family had stayed, Christina said, "I always wondered what that place is like inside."

"Quite nice."

"You've been there?"

"Yes."

"Luck-y," she said lightly. A few minutes later the airport—or what was left of it—came into view, and Christina sucked in a breath. "I know I was there, but…holy moly."

They pulled into the parking lot, mostly cleared of debris but now filled with assorted construction vehicles. He helped Christina out of the car, leaving a woefully disappointed Gumbo inside. The still, clear air reverberated with the off-sync banging of hammers and nail guns, a drill's high-pitched squeal. The ear-splitting "pop" of a power riveter. Sounds of hope and optimism and determination. In the distance he spotted Tanner Redmond, who acknowledged Scott with a wave of his hand.

Then, beside him, he heard Christina's low moan.

She hobbled over to what apparently had once been her car, now a mangled hunk of metal. Leaning on one crutch, she let go of the other long enough to lovingly stroke a brutal dent in the left fender.

"I'm so sorry," Scott said behind her.

Christina sniffed. "She lived a long, happy life. At least she was happy once I rescued her from the idiot teenager who'd abused her. Poor gal already had more than 200,000 miles on her at that point and her shocks were shot. But I nursed her back to health and she served me well for going on four years." She laid a cheek on the roof. "What an awful way to go. I'm so sorry, Ellie Mae."

Scott came up and put an arm around her shoulders. "If it's any consolation, I don't think she suffered," he said, and she gave a short laugh, then clamped her quivering lips together.

"What do you want to do? With the car, I mean?"

"I…I honestly don't know. Have it towed somewhere, I suppose…" Then, on a soft, strangled cry, she turned and buried her face in his chest.

"Hey…hey…" Wrapping her in his arms, he said, "It's okay, really…"

"Oh, yeah?" she mumbled into his jacket. "I didn't have comprehensive insurance. Couldn't afford it. And didn't figure the insurance company would give me more than a buck fifty for her, anyway." Watery eyes lifted to his. "So right now I have no job, no car and no way to get a car to get to a job." She pulled away, angrily swatting at her cheek with the heel of one hand. "Or any way to drive if I did have a car. So my usually upbeat outlook is sorta struggling right now."

His hands on her shoulders, Scott bent to look into her eyes. "You have your dog."

She looked over at Gumbo, doing his sad-sack look at her from the car window. "Not sure I'd get much for him as a trade-in, though—"

"And you have me," he said, and her eyes swung sharply back to his.

"Oh, no," she said, hooking her crutches under her arms and doing her Monster Mash lurch back to the Escalade. "I let you pay my E.R. bill, and pick up my dog's poop, but you are not buying me a car, no sir."

Scott easily caught up to her, opening the car door and helping her get settled inside. Then he stood with one hand on the door, the other propped on the roof.

"Actually, that hadn't occurred to me. I'd only meant I'd take care of the car so you wouldn't have to. But thanks for giving me the idea—"

"And you might not want to provoke an already aggravated woman with crutches at her disposal."

"I'll take my chances. Look, Christina…if it's so important to you, you can pick out whatever you feel comfortable with, then pay me back in installments when you do get a job. But we're going to get you another car. But lunch first, dammit, because I'm hungry." Then he slammed the door shut and stalked around to the driver's side, slamming that one shut, too, after he got back behind the wheel.

Silence engulfed them as they drove back to town. Even knowing Christina as little as he did, something told him this was not a good thing.

She was still miffed, frankly, by the time Scott eased the SUV into a space between a Mercedes and something else big and fancy and shiny in Red's parking lot. But more at herself than at him, for a boatload of conflicting reasons. For not knowing how to handle whatever this was between them with at least a modicum of grace. For realizing how easily she could let herself get sucked into the fairy tale. For liking the man even though she knew it was dumb and foolish and wrong, because he was caught up in the fairy tale, too, wasn't he? Playing the Prince to her Cinderella.

Then again, maybe she should simply accept the blessing and shut the heck up. Seize the day—and the car—and be grateful. Enjoy the moment while it lasted.

Scott opened her door, offered his hand. Glowered when she didn't immediately take it.

"Christina—"

"Once again, I'm sorry I'm acting like…whatever I'm acting like. But…but your coming along, acting like some fairy godfather…it makes me feel like that tornado got inside my head somehow, making an awful mess in there. So you're just going to have to be patient with me until everything settles down." She angled her head to peer up at him. "Okay?"

"Okay," he said after a moment. "Although I'm not sure I like the 'fairy' part of that description." But she was too busy gawking at the beautiful hacienda-turned-restaurant to pay him any mind.

"I'm not exactly dressed for this place, you know. I was thinking more along the lines of a drive-through burger and fries."

He hauled her to her good foot, his hand landing at the small of her back to steady her as his gaze took a leisurely stroll over her fitted pink hoodie, her ankle-length, tiered denim skirt, like she was wearing one of those fringed-and-sequined numbers from *Dancing with the Stars*. Oh, boy. Her foot might be broken, but everything else was apparently very much ready to rhumba.

"You're dressed fine," he said, his voice sounding a little raspy. "And I'd rather poke sharp sticks in my eyes than eat that crap."

"Snob."

"Not at all. But I would like to live past fifty." He left the window cracked for Gumbo, then steered her and her crutches toward the door. "And I'd like you to live past fifty, too."

It was a throwaway retort, she was sure. Didn't mean anything. And yet, her eyes stung. Dammit. All this time she'd done fine on her own without some ding-dong muddying the waters. Then *this* ding-dong comes along, flinging both his money and his pheromones left and right, and there goes all her hard work right down the drain.

Finally, Scott got her inside. Precariously balanced on the crutches, Christina glanced around, willing her eyes to adjust to the darkened interior and feeling every bit the rube.

"Two?" the smartly dressed hostess asked.

"Yes. And my friend needs to keep her foot up as much as possible, so if we could have a booth, or a table with an extra chair...?"

"Not a problem. Follow me."

The hostess led them to a table for four beside an arched window looking into a central courtyard anchored by several Mexican fan trees and dotted with pine tables and chairs, the brightly colored umbrellas over them mostly closed. Even in the sun it was a little chilly to dine outside, Christina guessed, but dormant vines still gracefully tangled around arbors, scrambled up support posts underneath the overhanging, clay-tiled roof. And in the center, an exquisite Mexican-tiled fountain softly gurgled and splashed, the soothing music audible even through the closed window.

Scott helped her get her foot propped up on the chair opposite, then sat at right angles to her, the ambient light glancing off his dark hair, his sharply defined jaw, as he studied the menu.

Terrific.

"This is very nice," she said, forcing her eyes to her own menu. Trying not to gasp at the prices. *Seize the moment, seize the—*

"You've never been here?"

She shook her head, then looked around, grateful to see she wasn't the only person dressed...casually. Then she giggled, pressing her hand to her mouth. "I'm sorry," she whispered, "but I can't help it, I feel like I'm playing grown-up."

Scott did that unsettling raking-her-with-his-eyes thing again—although not in a creepy way, at least—then said with a half smile, "You are very much a grown-up, Christina. Get used to it."

"Aw...do I gotta?"

His mouth twitching, Scott lowered his eyes to the menu. "Yes." She gave an exaggerated sigh, and his mouth twitched harder. Then he said, "What's your favorite color? To wear, I mean?"

"Color? I don't know, I've never really thought about it. Blues and turquoises, I suppose. Like the colors in those tiles," she said, indicating the fountain. "Why?"

He simply smiled, then nodded to her—like, you know, a gentleman?—when the peasant-bloused waitress appeared to take their orders. Christina gave hers—some grilled shrimp dish that sounded amazing—then mused, as she listened to Scott give his, that it was a good thing she was done with men, since this dude was totally going to spoil her for anybody else.

A thought that didn't give her nearly as much satisfaction as she'd hoped.

Clearly, Scott thought, amused, as he watched tiny little Christina chow down her lunch like a linebacker, if he wanted her to open up, all he had to do was feed her.

Not that the conversation was personal to any real degree. At least on her end. She still avoided discussing her past, deftly sidestepping any questions that might lead to answers she clearly didn't want to give. Although instinct told him she simply wanted to avoid pain more than, say, jail time, a more guarded woman he'd never met. Which provoked as much admiration as annoyance.

About her private life, at least. Because about everything else—from politics to world affairs to their favorite movies—she had no qualms whatsoever about locking his gaze into hers as she leaned over her plate, her hands going a mile a minute to emphasize her point. There was little she wasn't interested in—or didn't have a fervently expressed opinion about—and the longer the meal went on, the more Scott became aroused, by her intelligence, her quick wit, the way her cheeks pinked when she got excited.

By that adorable little crease that kept playing peeka-boo with her forehead. She was simply…amazing. And the most amazing thing about it was that she had no idea how amazing she was. She made him think, she made him laugh, she made him feel like doing a Gene Kelly number. With an umbrella. In the rain. And every minute he spent with her made him realize even more what an idiot he'd be to let her go.

That *this* was what all the fuss was about.

Now if he could just figure out how to overcome those pesky trust issues, he'd be set—

Not for the first time during the meal, his phone buzzed. Carefully drizzling honey into a sopapilla, Christina nodded toward it. "You can go ahead and get that, you know. Doesn't bother me in the least."

"It's rude."

"Not if it's okay with me. Scott…I know you're a busy man. As it is, I can't figure out how you're pulling this off. You've left your life to be here…that can't be easy."

No, I've found *my life,* he wanted to say. Except why ruin the good mood? So all he said was, "A lot easier than you might think." When she frowned, he added, "This is the first time I've…" He caught himself before he said, *been on a date,* figuring that would not go over well. "I've shared a meal with someone where my phone wasn't the third person at the table. Not only did my companions not appreciate it, I didn't enjoy it, either. Believe me, multitask-ing is highly overrated."

She gave him more of that steady gaze, then said, "You know, you sound tired. I don't mean physically—"

"No, I know what you mean. And you're right, I am.

For once in my life I'd like to focus on one thing and savor it, rather than three or four and not enjoy any of them. And right now," he said, grasping her free hand, "I'm here, having lunch with you, and enjoying the heck out of it. So can I have my moment, please?"

For several seconds her eyes held his, as sharp and discerning as an old woman's. "Sure," she said, at last, her smile relaxing more than it had yet, and his heart seized up so hard and fast he nearly flinched. Wendy was right, he had it bad.

Speaking of his sister...

"By the way," he said, releasing Christina's hand, "Wendy suggested you might like to come help her make decorating decisions about her nursery."

"Oh, Scott..." Her eyes lowered, she removed her napkin, painstakingly refolding it before tucking it underneath the rim of her plate. Then her mouth twisted into a funny little smile, the same one she'd given him when he'd first mentioned his sister. "What do I know about decorating?"

"Knowing Wendy, I imagine she used the term *help* very loosely. Basically, I think she's looking for a yes-man. Or in this case, woman. So will you do it? Might do both of you good. And I think...she could use a friend."

He'd stopped short of saying he thought *Christina* could use a friend, even if it was true. Because right now it was patently clear the woman sitting across from him needed to regain her footing, in more ways than one. And one of those, he surmised, was by feeling needed. Useful.

"Maybe in a few days," she finally said, the smile reappearing. "When I'm feeling more...myself."

"Good deal," he said, gesturing to the waitress for the check. "Now where's the best place to shop for a car around here?"

"San Antonio. But, Scott—I can't even drive yet—"

"Strike while the iron's hot, I always say." The credit card slip signed, he got to his feet. "And I'm in the mood to buy something. You might want to take advantage of that."

She gave him a look that could either have been indulgent or exasperated. Then she sighed, and there was no doubt at all what *that* meant.

"I'm sorry," he said, "I don't mean to push you—"

"Like you're not hardwired to do exactly that. And if I told you no, flat out, that I don't want you buying me a car, you'd probably do it anyway. Right?"

"Can I admit I'd at least be tempted?"

Her mouth pulled flat. Definitely exasperated. "What am I going to do with you?"

"Let me buy you a car?" he said, and she gave a weary laugh, those sweet eyes finally touching his.

"Will it really make you happy?"

He came around to help her stand, trying to figure out why the scent of her drugstore shampoo should wreak such havoc on his senses. Let alone his common sense. Because what would make him happy right now wasn't anything they could do in Red, that was for damn sure.

Nor was there any way he could tell her a few thousand dollars meant nothing to him and not come across like some ego-bloated braggart who assumed money could buy him any woman he wanted.

So all he said was, "Yes. It would make me very happy. Will that work for you?"

"I guess it'll have to, won't it?" she said, then started toward the door.

Somehow he thought victory was supposed to feel sweeter than this.

Chapter Seven

Christina sat on the porch in the warm afternoon sun, her leg propped up, staring at the pretty little VW Jetta. Silver. Three years old, barely twenty thousand miles on it. A week on and she still couldn't believe it was hers.

Which only added to the rapidly growing list of things she was having a hard time believing. Like Scott's still being here after two weeks. Not to mention her sorta getting used to letting him do stuff for her. Without feeling guilty about it, even. Or at least not as much.

Beside her, in an original-edition webbed lawn chair, Enid grunted. "I cannot believe you let the man buy you a car."

Which the older woman had only said a million times since she'd first seen it sitting in the parking lot. And with no less vexation in her voice now than the first time. Never mind that she'd told Christina yesterday that Scott had paid up her rent three months in advance. Or that he'd ferried

Enid to Walmart right after. Both on the sly, of course. Honestly, Christina never knew whether to hug or strangle the man. Or strangle herself. On the upside, at least there'd been no more silly talk about her past. Or those "real" feelings he'd mentioned a week ago. 'Cause for sure *somebody'd* be dead by now if there had been.

"Well, I did. And don't tell me you can't wait until I drive you to your hair appointment in it."

"It does look like a very nice car, I gotta admit. So where's Lover Boy today?"

"I don't know and don't call him that. He said he had some things to take care of. I didn't figure it was any of my business to ask what."

"He going back home soon?"

Her heart knocking in her chest, Christina looked over to where Gumbo was rustling around in the underbrush, looking for something to chase. Or pee on. "I suppose."

"You don't know?"

"Don't see how that's any of my business, either," she said, and Enid grunted. "By the way, did I tell you? I registered to take online classes for the next semester, so I don't have to worry about getting to campus. I also did some research and found this website that matches up tutors with kids who need help with basic skills. We can either work together in person or on Skype."

"What's that?"

"This cool computer hookup where you can see the person you're talking to. You know that jewelry commercial where the guy overseas is talking to his wife and son? That's Skype."

"Oh." Then her landlady shook her head. "I swear, things move too damn fast for me to keep up."

Christina laughed. "Don't feel bad. Even I feel as if technology changes every five minutes. Anyway, soon as the outfit that runs the program finishes up my background check to make sure I'm okay to work with kids, I'll have a job. And one that pays a lot better than waitressing at the airport ever did, that's for sure. And why are you looking at me like that?"

"Because you are one of the smartest gals I ever met, and that's a fact."

"Hardly—"

"And don't you go acting all modest on me. It's true. I mean, look at you—instead of wallowing in your troubles, you figure out how to solve your problems. You are something else, young lady—"

"Hey. I wallowed. I wallowed plenty."

"For, what? A week?" She blew a dismissive *pfhh* through her lips.

"And if Scott hadn't jumped in to help with the medical expenses, and the car—"

"Yeah, yeah, I know, but that's all the immediate stuff. What you did, that's taking care of the future. Did Lover Boy have anything to do with that?"

"Well, no, but—"

"Then just accept the damn compliment, will you?" Over Christina's chuckle, Enid added, "You know, I'm gonna miss you like nobody's business when you leave."

Christina's head snapped around. "Leave? No way. Red Rock's my home, Enid. Where I belong. Unless you got a crystal ball in your pocket that knows something I don't."

"No, but I've been around a lot longer than you, which means I'm real good at readin' people. You ain't even begun to reach your full potential, and…and you don't need to be letting some man derail you, neither, making you all starry-eyed and whatnot and then first thing you know you can't remember the last time you did something for yourself. You got things to do, missy, even if you don't know yet what those are…and now why are you laughing at me?"

"Because you're not telling me anything I don't already know. In case you forgot. You bet I've got things to do, but there's nothing saying I can't do them right here in Red Rock. Or close by, anyway. I'm not about to let a man mess with my head, believe me." She thought about the look in Scott's eyes that night, like he would've liked nothing more than to sweep her off to Atlanta to turn her into a proper Southern lady. A thought that made her shudder. "Or take me places I don't want to go." Then she said, "You don't like Scott, do you?"

"Ain't got nothing to do with liking the boy. I like him just fine. He's good folks, far as I can tell. But it ain't me he's courting, is it?"

"He's not *courting* me, either—"

"The hell he ain't. And a man like that, he can be hard to resist. Make a gal forget what she's about, what she's got to do. Nothin' against Scott. I just want you to be sure."

"Of what?"

"Of whatever you need to be sure about."

Christina looked away. "No worries. Promise."

"Well. Okay, then," her landlady said with a sharp shake of her head that did not so much as disturb a single hair on it. "Got a cleaning crew coming in a bit, you know Marlene and her kids moved out of number 5, right? Left the place in a right mess, too. Least she didn't stiff me for the last month's rent like so many of 'em do, but it's gonna cost me near that much to get the place back in decent shape…" She stopped, her lips pulled thin. "I love you, girl, you know that, right?"

Tears pricked at Christina's eyes. "I love you, too, Enid. But I'm okay. Promise."

Which she sternly told herself after Enid left and she

saw the Escalade turn into the parking lot, and her heart ka-thumped so hard in her chest it nearly made her burp. She hadn't been expecting him, even though he'd shown up every single day. Sometimes twice. But *expecting* him— expecting *anything*—would have been foolish, and she liked to think she'd outgrown foolish a long time ago.

Gumbo, of course, bounded over to the car before Scott had even cut the engine, all flapping ears and wagging everything. Because dogs had no pride. Or inhibitions. You love somebody, you let him know. Simple. To the point.

And when Scott finally disentangled himself from Gumbo's totally inappropriate PDA and lifted his eyes to Christina's, she thought—with a sharp pang—how much easier it would be to be a dog. To simply love because that's what you did, with no regard for the consequences. Or worry about potential heartbreak.

But she wasn't a dog. She was a human being whose brain and heart—and body, no point leaving that out of the equation—were at severe odds with each other right now. Because for all that she really was grateful he hadn't *said* anything more, she got the real strong feeling the issue had not, by any means, been laid to rest.

And right now? Watching Scott Fortune cross toward her like he owned the whole state, his eyes fixed on hers in the way of a man who clearly had hanky-panky on his mind?

It wasn't the fantasy scaring the bejeebers out of her.

It was the reality.

She was giving him the same look she always did, a fake aloofness she had no clue how to pull off with any degree of conviction.

Oh, he had no doubt her resistance was sincere, that there were real reasons behind the ambivalence haunting her eyes, her blatant avoidance of any prolonged physical contact. She was clearly leery, although whether of him or relationships in general, he still had no idea.

And over the past week, that had begun to worry him more and more. Not her wariness, but the very real danger that…she might be onto something. That the thrill of the challenge might be motivating his interest far more than he wanted to admit. After all, Christina was one smart cookie. And when *had* he last pursued any sort of relationship— business or pleasure—that didn't serve his self-interest in some way?

Did he even know how to have a relationship for its own sake? To be with someone simply because he wanted to be with her? Was his almost constant ache for Christina—the bad timing on that notwithstanding—simply because it'd been a while, or because he genuinely ached for *her?*

"What's up?" she asked, her obvious attempt to keep things light twisting his heart. The pansies nodded at him as he approached, the gentle breeze easing through his Oxford shirt, teasing strands of pale gold across Christina's cheeks. Her lightweight top was a field of softly blurred flowers, blues and lavenders and deep pinks, lazily strewn across her shoulders. Her breasts. Very feminine. Very her.

"Thought you might like to meet Wendy today," he said, suddenly realizing exactly how much he wanted to pulverize that wall keeping her locked inside herself…and then shield her from whatever had made her erect that wall to begin with.

At which moment he also realized exactly how groundless his earlier worries were. Oh, yeah, he was in it to win it, no question. But because he wanted *her,* not because he wanted to win.

"She said the decorator left a bunch of swatches," he continued, as though all hell wasn't breaking loose inside his head. "The two of you could have lunch together, I'll pick you up later."

Confusion flickered in her eyes. "You won't be there?"

"No, I've got…some business to attend to."

"Oh. Well, then…" A smile bloomed across her face. "Sure. Why not?"

"And bring the dog. Wendy wants to meet him, too."

When he opened the rear door, however, for her to climb into the back seat, she shook her head. "The swelling's all gone. I'd like to sit in front, if you don't mind?"

"Not at all."

Once again, getting out seemed to relax her. Her enthusiasm contagious, she told him all about her signing up for online classes, her potential job.

"So you like working with kids?"

She nodded, her gaze fixed out the windshield. "I love kids. What about you?"

"I think kids are the neatest things going. The way their minds work—slays me every time."

Her eyes cut briefly to his. "So…any plans to make a bunch of baby Fortunes?"

"Don't know about a bunch…but I suppose so. Although, to be honest, I hadn't really given it much thought until recently."

"Oh, yeah? What made you change your mind?"

"I never said I was opposed to the idea, it's just…" His fist tightened around the steering wheel. "Since getting married wasn't on my radar, neither was having kids. Then we came out here for Wendy's wedding, and she's pregnant and happy and…"

"And you got all broody."

"I suppose."

Several seconds ticked by before Christina said, "Betcha

there's a whole slew of gals in Atlanta who'd be thrilled to hear that."

Scott pushed out a dry laugh. "No doubt," he said, nosing into his sister's driveway beside a hedge of rangy, unclipped euonymus. "And here we are. It was Marcos's before they got married. As you can tell, yard work isn't exactly a top priority…no, wait, let me help you—"

"Nope, got it," Christina said, pushing open the door, grabbing her crutches from behind his seat and hauling her adorable little bottom out of the car the same moment Gumbo scrambled out behind her. When Scott reached her, she laughed. "Get me, huh?"

I'd love to, he thought as Wendy waddled outside, looking like a shiny red balloon in her stretchy top. Then Scott noticed his sister's way-too-high, rope-soled shoes…about the same time Christina did.

"Ohmigosh—those shoes are awesome!" she said, moving much more gracefully with the crutches than she had even a few days ago.

"Thanks!" Wendy said, awkwardly twisting around to show off the three-inch heel, then bending over—sort of—to pet Gumbo. "These are my favorites, I can't fit my fat feet into anything else these days! And aren't you the cutest thing going?" she said to the dog, who'd already propped his pudgy feet on her thighs to get some love. Then Wendy turned her smile on Christina. "Well, come on in, I've already got lunch on the table, Scott's told me so much about you—"

"I'll be back in a couple of hours," Scott called, but they were already inside.

Laughing softly to himself as he walked back around to the driver's side, he pulled out his cell phone and punched in the number already on speed dial. "I can meet you out there in ten minutes," he said, climbing in behind the wheel and backing out of the driveway.

He still hadn't decided if he'd lost his mind or finally found it. He did know that whichever that was, none of this was going to be easy. He knew what he wanted, was pretty sure he knew why, but from this point forward it was all uncharted territory.

But as he sped down the highway, his grin stretched his face so hard it hurt.

"You don't think the colors are too much?"

Grinning at the blinding array of tropical hues splayed out on the nursery's carpet, Christina shook her head. A few feet away Gumbo snoozed in a puddle of sunlight, ears akimbo. "I love them. Especially this for the drapes," she said, holding up the bold, contemporary floral print, orange and fuchsia and lemon-yellow flowers on a bright aqua background. Christina sat on the floor, her healing foot stretched out in front of her, while Wendy held court from the aqua-and-white glider already in place in the corner, her feet planted on a matching ottoman.

"The furniture and walls are all going to be white," Wendy said, "so I figured I could go a little crazy with the rest of it. And I've already hired an artist to come paint a border of the same flowers on the opposite wall." Then she laughed. "When I was little, my room was princess pink. Every square inch of it. It was like waking up every morning inside a glob of cotton candy."

Christina smiled, the image mercifully blotting out the memories. She seriously doubted if Wendy could even fathom what some of Christina's sleeping arrangements had been like. "Were your sisters' rooms pink, too?"

"Heavens, no. Emily's was all yellows and creams, and Jordana's was pale blue. Of course, they might have been pink at the start, but that didn't last long. Any more than it did with me," she said with another giggle. "I marched into my parents' room on my tenth birthday and announced I wanted a red room. Or else."

"Oh, dear. How did that go over?"

"Oh, I got my red room, all right. Except then I started having nightmares about vampires attacking me in my sleep. So I ended up with a nice, soft periwinkle."

"Sounds perfect." Christina skootched back to rest her back against the wall, itching—literally—to remove the cast. "And...your brothers? What were their rooms like?"

"Typical boy, I suppose, I never paid much attention. And I was still really small when Mike and Scott went off to college and Mom turned both of their rooms into guestrooms. Very Atlanta traditional, dark wood furniture, striped wallpaper, floral bedspreads." She made a face. "Tasteful but boring. Blake's, though—I remember his, since I spent so much time in it. Über high tech. A fish tank large enough to hold a shark. Okay, a small shark... hey. You okay?"

Jerking up her head, Christina nodded, not about to let on that listening to Wendy talk about the family had taken her back to those hours she'd spent trapped with Scott after the tornado. Despite their wealth, in many ways the Fortunes sounded like your average American family, some of the bonds between various members stronger than others. Still and all, what they had—and she didn't mean their money—was far more than she could've even imagined—

"I'm fine, I just wonder where Scott is." At Wendy's raised brows, she smiled. "You must be very ready for me to go home by now."

"Don't kid yourself. This is the most fun I've had in ages. I cannot wait until this little peanut is outside and I can walk more than three feet without getting winded. And drive. Nobody tells you when you're short that if you adjust the steering wheel so it doesn't stab you in the stomach, your feet won't reach the pedals!"

But the young woman's can't-hold-it-in happiness certainly tempered the moaning and groaning. Yes, more than a few vestiges of her privileged upbringing still clung to her—the baby girl's nursery was not being done on the cheap, nor were the silver bangles that softly clinked every time Wendy gestured with her left hand, Christina didn't imagine—but all the trappings couldn't hide the real sweetheart underneath. Wendy, too, was "good folks," as Enid liked to say.

Then Wendy said, "You mind if I ask you something?" and a faint prickle of alarm tracked up Christina's spine.

"Depends on what that is, I suppose."

Rubbing her belly, Wendy glanced out the window to the backyard beyond, then returned her gaze to Christina, a tiny wrinkle etched between her dark brows. "Did something…happen between you and my brother when y'all were trapped together after the tornado?"

Christina's face flamed. "What—what do you mean?"

"I'm not sure. That's why I'm asking. And I know the question sounds totally out of line…" She huffed out a sigh, then a little laugh. "I know it's not possible, but I swear sometimes it feels as if the baby's pushed everything inside me all the way up into my brain! But if you'd known Scott before…"

She wagged her head. "Everything he did, even when he dated, it all felt so…controlled. Calculated. I never once saw him do something on the spur of the moment. I mean, okay, so all my brothers and sisters live, eat and breathe that business. Just like Daddy. But I always got the feeling Scott was like that because he thought he had to be. Not because that's who he really was."

Christina picked up a fabric swatch again, smoothing it over her thigh. "And now you think something's changed?"

"Oh, I know something's changed. There's a light in his eyes I don't ever remember seeing before. Only thing is, I can't quite tell what's put it there."

Lifting her eyes—and running smack dab into Wendy's pointed look—Christina nervously laughed. "And you think it's me?"

A devilish grin spread across the young woman's cheeks. "Can't think of another reason why he's still here. Blake says Daddy's about to have five fits that Scott's not home yet."

And you're young and in love and running on pregnancy hormones, Christina thought, not unkindly. Because maybe only a few years separated them, but what Christina lacked in privilege and wealth she more than made up for in experience—a treasury that easily trumped the younger woman's a hundredfold.

"Even if that was true," she said carefully, "no way would I come between him and his father. Because I've been there before, and it wasn't pretty."

"Oooh…" Wendy's brows lifted. "I'm guessing there's a story behind that comment."

There was—a long, sorry one—but Christina had already said more than she should have. Through the open window she heard the SUV pull into the driveway. Praise be.

"Nothing worth resurrecting," she said lightly, hauling herself to her feet and grabbing her crutches at the same time Wendy got to hers and pulled Christina into a hug.

"Listen, I can be a good friend," she said, her expression earnest. "I also know how to keep my mouth shut. What I'm saying is…you need somebody to talk to, I'm your girl.

But I swear on my life not one word would get back to Scott if you don't want it to."

Oddly, Christina believed her. Or at least she believed Wendy's good intentions. But she'd been that route before, too. So all she did was hug her back and thank her for the offer, just in time to look up and catch Scott's bewildered expression from the nursery doorway.

"What was that all about?" Scott asked mildly after they were on the road again. Christina frowned over at him. "I heard you thank her for her offer."

"Oh." She faced front again. "To…give me some of her recipes."

"You are one lousy liar, you know that?"

She was quiet for a moment, then said, "Not to be rude or anything, but it was girl stuff, okay? No boys allowed. So…did you have a successful afternoon?"

The gentle, but firm, rebuke hit its mark. Although considering he wasn't ready to come clean to her yet, either, this time he could hardly fault the woman for playing her cards close to her chest.

"Not entirely, no. But there's always tomorrow." And yet, when she didn't say anything—in other words, didn't play the game the way he wanted it played—it mildly ticked him off. "Aren't you even remotely curious?"

"Not even remotely," she said. Staring *really* hard out the window.

That's my girl, he thought, grinning. "As I said. Lousy liar."

She scratched the side of her nose, then tightly folded her arms across her ribs. "Bein' curious and thinking you have the right to pry into somebody's private business are two different things. Especially when that business has nothing to do with you."

"What makes you think it doesn't?"

The car bumped over some debris in the road. "In that case, I *really* don't want to know."

Scott chuckled. "You are one strange bird, you know that?"

"Never said I wasn't…why are we turning off here?"

"Don't you recognize it?"

"Well, yeah, it's where the old barn used to be, but—"

"Then you probably know there's a pretty little stand of pines by a pond on the other side of the property. It's a beautiful day—I thought you might like to go sit by it for a bit."

She looked like a little girl being teased by somebody holding a favorite doll out of her reach. "Whoever owns the land might not take kindly to us trespassing, you know."

"The owner's in New Mexico. Has been for twenty years. I doubt she'd care."

"How do you know all this?"

"I make it my business to know these things. What is it they say about nature abhorring a vacuum? So does my brain."

"You do realize how scary that sounds?"

"Does it scare you?"

After a moment's apparent contemplation, she shook her head. "Not especially."

This time he didn't call her on the fib. Especially since, this time, he wasn't amused. Odd, how all his adult life he'd worked the intimidation factor, figuring if a little fear got him where he wanted to go, it was all well and good. Even in his personal life—the minute he felt a woman was getting too comfortable, felt his control of the relationship slipping, she was history. But it was different with Christina. *He* was different. The idea of her being afraid of him, even a little, made him sick to his stomach. Sure, he still wanted what he wanted, but what he wanted…

Was for her to want him, too. Every bit as badly as he did her.

On her terms. Not his.

He drove the SUV to the end of the dirt road, Gumbo bursting from the backseat the instant Scott opened the door to bound across the field like the jackrabbits he probably hoped to find. Then, an old blanket purloined from Marcos's car in hand, he helped Christina out. Her eyes grazed his for a moment, questioning, before she turned away. Shielding her eyes from the sun, she scanned the landscape, bright gold under a clear, cloudless sky. And let out a long, slow breath.

"Now this is what you call pure Texas," she said. "Standing here, with all this sky and sun…it's like being reborn."

He couldn't have said it better himself. Smiling, Scott let his gaze wander further west, over the sweet seven hundred or so acres nobody but he—and his Realtor—knew he had an eye on. And until it was a done deal nobody else was going to know he'd finally made the decision that would change everything.

"Come on, sit," he said, shaking out the blanket and smoothing it over a bed of needles underneath one of the pines. Christina sat, folding up one leg to hug her knee while Scott stretched out beside her on his side, propped up on one elbow. In the distance, Gumbo let out a happy bark, bounced into view as if to say *I'm okay, Mom, see?* then bounced off again.

"So you gonna tell me the real reason why you brought me here?"

"Just thought you'd like it. That's all."

"Apparently I'm not the only one who's a lousy liar."

Scott plucked at a pine needle that had blown onto the

blanket, twirling it in his fingers. "If I told you how much I'd like to kiss you right now," he said, "would you be a, flattered, b, annoyed or c, ambivalent?"

"What is this, one of those questions on OkCupid?"

He looked up at her. "You've been on a dating site?" To his immense delight, she blushed.

"Never you mind about that—"

"Answer the question."

"What's *annoying* is that I can't simply get up and stomp off right now."

He grinned. "Yeah. I know."

On a groan, she dropped her head onto her folded-up hands, then lifted it again, staring off into the distance. "Scott…you don't want to kiss *me*."

"I sure don't want to kiss Gumbo."

She laughed softly, then said, "No, I mean…you want to kiss who you think I am. Or who you think I could be. Take your pick."

"And you think *my* brain is scary?" He reached up to curl his fingers around her hand. "Honey, I—"

"Now, see?" she said, pulling her hand from his. "You can stop right there with your 'honeys' and 'sweethearts' and 'trust mes.' Because they're nothing more than words a man uses to make a woman think things she has no business thinking."

Scott felt his forehead pinch. "And what is it you're so sure you have no business thinking?"

"Not important," she said, even as Scott thought, *Says who?* "But…but your sister said she thinks everything that happened with the tornado and the aftermath, it all messed with your head, somehow. That you're acting different from what she's used to. No, wait, let me finish."

After a little rustling around she stretched out next to him, mirroring his position, eyes locked in his. Her hair had worked loose, tumbling in soft waves around her shoulder. "I'm not saying it didn't. In fact, I have no business saying otherwise, seeing as it messed with my head, too. Big-time. But if anything it made me see things more clearly. Made me more sure of what I wanted. What I needed. But you…"

Sighing, she rolled onto her back, her hands resting on her stomach. "From everything your sister tells me, it sounds like you've been focused so hard on your work all these years that you lost sight of *you* somewhere along the way."

She angled her head to look at him. "Then this crazy storm comes along and shakes you up. Throws everything out of whack. But the thing about storms is, eventually they end. And when they do, you look around and realize…everything's messed up. Not new. Not better. Just… messed up. Maybe I'm different from every other woman you've ever known, but that doesn't mean our getting stuck together was some kind of sign. All of this…it's a novelty to you, Scott. I'm a novelty. Or a project, I haven't quite decided which yet. So I meant what I said, about you not really wanting to kiss me. Because you're only seeing who you want to see. Not who I really am."

Scott looked at her for a long time, then said, "You could have just said 'no.'"

She blinked. "About what?"

"This," he said, then closed the few inches between them and lowered his mouth to hers.

Chapter Eight

There were, Christina knew, hot kisses and mediocre kisses and kisses so boring you found yourself contemplating what was on TV that night. But never, not even during that period of her life she thought about as little as possible, had she ever experienced a kiss like this.

Oh, my, yes, she thought, as Scott wrapped his hand around her neck, possessive and gentle and warm, angling their mouths to go deeper, *this* kiss was in a category all its own.

This kiss was Ferris wheels and warm summer breezes and spinning around and around with your arms held wide until you fell over, dizzy and laughing. Bubbles of delight scurried along her skin, through her blood, making things tingle and curl and sweetly ache and her brain feel like it'd exploded into a thousand sparkly bits underneath her skull.

Scott broke the kiss and eased away, his fingers toying with the hair at her temple, the lopsided grin on his face making her want to smack him. And/or kiss him all over again.

And she thought she'd been in trouble *before*.

"I never did answer your question, you know," she said, her heart whomping so hard against her sternum it almost hurt.

"I took a gamble," he said, still grinning. "And I think I can safely say that first kiss? Wasn't a fluke. Or terror-driven."

Apparently worn out from his exploits, Gumbo trotted up and wedged himself between them, exhilarated and panting. Scott let go of Christina to scratch the dog's head.

"The kiss was okay," she said, sitting up again. Frantically searching for her composure. If not her common sense.

"Like hell." Scott sat up as well, cupping her jaw to bring her face back around to his. Thinking he was gonna kiss her again—and not at all sure how she felt about that—Christina sucked in a breath. But all he did was stroke his thumb across her cheek, over and over, and stare into her eyes like he all but knew she was hiding something in there.

She looked away. "Don't."

Because she was. All kinds of things she didn't talk about, ever, because they hurt too much. Made her feel weak and vulnerable and dumb all over again. Or worse, would make him feel sorrier for her than she suspected he already did. And that was one card she refused to play.

He dropped his hand. "I have no intention of hurting you, Christina."

"I'm sure you don't. Doesn't mean you won't." She grabbed her crutches. "Can we leave now? My foot's beginning to give me fits."

Another lie. And he probably knew it. But she desperately needed to get back to reality, to what she knew. What she could control.

Nodding, Scott helped her up.

Neither said a single word the whole way back to her place. Until, when they turned into the complex's parking lot, Christina spotted her mother's bright red Ford Fiesta parked next to her new car. And, on her porch, the woman herself, all decked out in a too-low top, too-tight pants and too-big hair.

"Your mother?" Scott said beside her as he pulled up.

"None else. Although why she's here I couldn't tell you."

"To make sure you're okay?"

Christina reached around to grab her crutches from the back seat, briefly meeting Scott's eyes. "After two weeks? The saying 'day late and a dollar short' comes to mind."

She waited until he'd come around to help her out. Pride was one thing. Making herself look like a blamed fool was something else again. But before he offered her his hand, he leaned close enough to say, "You don't have to face this alone. Not if you don't want to."

Gumbo leapt out and waggled over to her mother, who jumped up with her hands in the air, screeching. "Call your dog, Christina—oh, for heaven's sake, get *down!*"

"I can handle my mother, Scott. And besides…"

"You want me to leave."

Once again, their eyes met. And, oh, dear God in heaven, did she want to believe what she saw in them. But how could she when she doubted he truly believed it, either? "I *need* you to leave. Red Rock, if at all possible."

For the first time, she saw something like doubt flicker in his eyes. "Do you really mean that?"

"Does it matter? Scott," she said quickly when he looked away, "I'm not deliberately trying to piss you off. I'm more grateful than I can say for everything you've done for me, but I have to be realistic. Why can't you understand that?"

Several strained seconds passed before Scott walked around to the driver's side, got in and drove off. If the universe had a shred of decency, that would be the last time she saw him.

Never mind that the thought of never experiencing another kiss like that made facing her mother sound delightful in comparison.

Speaking of whom...

"I wondered where you'd gotten off to," Sandra said, patting down her thighs where Gumbo had left dusty footprints.

At her door, Christina dug her keys out of her jeans' pocket. "Sorry. Were you waiting long?"

"Almost a half hour."

The door opened, Christina let her mother inside first, then stomped in after her and shut the door, immediately feeling like all the air had been sucked out of the room. "You should've called. If I'd known you were coming I would've made sure I was here."

"It wasn't planned. I had to go into San Antonio and thought I may as well drop in, since it was on the way. Especially since I had to use the toilet and you now how I hate public restrooms." Of course. And with that, Sandra vanished into Christina's bathroom, emerging a scant two minutes later, glancing around the apartment without really looking at Christina. "So I guess you're getting on okay?"

"Sure. Thanks for asking."

Her mother's lips pursed. "That the same young man who was at the hospital? The Fortune fella?"

"Scott. Yes. Would you like something to drink?"

"Sweet tea, if you have it. And I cannot believe you're going down this path again."

Ditching the crutches long enough to pull the tea pitcher out of the fridge, Christina felt her jaw clench. "I'm not going down any path, Mama. Scott's been very kind to me, is all." She poured her mother her tea, setting the tumbler on the tiny dining table.

"Kind enough to buy you that car?"

"Yes, if you must know."

"Oh, Christina…"

"It wasn't like I asked him. In fact, I told him not to. He insisted."

"Because he's trying to get into your pants, no doubt."

"No, because he's a kind, decent, generous man," she said, turning so her mother wouldn't see her blush. Not that she thought for a minute Scott's motives were solely…that. But she'd be a fool to believe the subject hadn't been hovering between them, especially after that kiss. What would frost her mother, though, was how little Christina would mind the prospect. Even knowing it would be—or would have been—strictly one of those for-the-moment things.

"And I can't believe you didn't learn your lesson the first time—"

"Mama! Stop. Now."

"I'm only saying—"

"I learned, okay?" Christina said, refusing to listen to her stinging eyes. Because while Enid's lectures stemmed, she knew, from genuine concern, her mother's hailed from that bottomless pit of self-interest that had motivated her every comment, her every action, for as long as Christina could remember. "Oh, boy, did I learn. So nothing's happening between Scott and me. And it's not going to. And you know, you've got some nerve coming here and butting into my personal life when you couldn't even be bothered to drive me home when I got out of the hospital."

"You don't get to talk to me like that," Sandra said,

pushing herself up from the table. "After everything I've done for you, raising you all alone—"

"*Done* for me? Are you serious? Here's a newsflash, Mama—*you* don't get to be a mother only when it's convenient. Or when it suits your purpose." On a roll now, Christina pointed to the door. "That man, who you're so all-fired convinced is only after one thing? He's paid more attention to me in the last two weeks than you have in the past five *years*. Frankly, if he did want to get in my pants? I'd let him, gladly. Because he's *earned* it, dammit!"

Her mother looked like her hair was going to catch fire. Which would only be an improvement. "You don't mean that."

Christina blew out a long, rough sigh. "Fine, even if he were sticking around, I'm not going to jump the man's bones. But everything else? Every single word."

"He's not staying?"

So much for making her point. "Of course not. His work, his whole life, is in Atlanta. So, see? The whole thing's moot."

Her mother looked at her for a long, hard moment. "I never realized how much you hated me."

"I don't hate you, Mama," Christina said, wearily. "But I don't understand you. Why you are the way you are. Why you've always treated me like I was an afterthought. That makes me sad, and more than a little angry, but it is what it is."

After another long look, her mother traipsed to the door and let herself out. Exhausted, Christina collapsed into the sofa, Gumbo immediately hopping up to smush up against her side and lay his head on her knee.

"Guess it's just you and me, boy," she said. "Like always."

Then, much to her disgust, she burst into tears.

* * *

On hearing Wendy's laugh from the living room when Scott walked into the house, Scott hesitated, not wanting to interrupt a private conversation. Until he realized she was talking to his youngest brother. He found her stretched out on the black leather couch with her phone pressed to her ear while playing remote roulette with her other hand.

"I'm fine, I promise…and speak of the devil." Angling the phone, she said, "Blake's asking if you know when you're coming home yet."

Sighing, Scott reached for the phone, carrying it into the kitchen so Wendy could watch her fashion-makeover show in peace, wiggling her bare, unpainted toes as she nibbled on a bowl of trail mix.

Scott slid onto a barstool at the counter dividing the kitchen from the small dining room, massaging the bridge of his nose. "Hey."

"Hey, yourself. You told Dad a week. It's been two. And from everything Wendy said, it sounds as though things are under control as far as Javier's concerned. As much as they can be, at least. You do remember you have a job here, right?"

Letting his hand drop to the laminate surface, Scott stared across the serviceable but woefully outdated room, listening to the benign hum of the white refrigerator. *A job.* Funny to think that he'd poured ten years' worth of time and energy into something that, when all was said and done, was just that: a job. Not a career or a calling, but…a job, his shares of the business as a family member notwithstanding.

No time like the present, he supposed, to come clean.

"I'm not coming back, Blake."

Stunned silence vibrated in his ear, followed by, "You can't be serious."

"I've never been more serious in my life. Mike can continue to handle whatever's on my desk—since most of it came from him, anyway—or it can be divvied up among the others. That guy who filled in for me last year when I was in Europe? He's ripe for promotion, anyway, hand some of it to him—"

"Whoa, dude—what have you been smoking? You can't simply…walk away."

"Watch me."

"Holy crap. Does Dad know?"

"Not yet. And not a word. I'll deal with him soon enough."

Blake snorted. "Not to worry. You can drop that little bombshell yourself. But…why?"

"Because when I was lying underneath half an airport's worth of rubble, it occurred to me life's too damn short to spend it doing something simply because it's what's expected of you. That I've worked my ass off for ten years pursuing somebody else's dream. Not going to do that anymore."

"I don't understand. You've always been so gung-ho about the business, working harder than any of us, except maybe Mike. Are you saying it was all a lie?"

"No," Scott said on a breath. "I wasn't faking it. Then again, I was also too busy to realize there were other options. Options that might actually make me smile when I get up in the morning."

Blake released a nervous laugh. "This is crazy, Scott."

"No guts, no glory." *Or peace,* he silently added.

"So…what's the plan?"

"You know me, never talk about a work in progress until it's a done deal."

"Ah. This…wouldn't have anything to do with that girl, would it? Christine?"

"Christina," Scott said softly. "And since I can only imagine what Wendy's already told you, there's not much point in denying it."

Blake let out a long, low whistle. "Ho-lee crap, Scott. You're in *love?*"

Scott abandoned the stool to pace in front of the dining table, one hand clamped around the back of his neck. There was that question again, demanding he quit sidestepping the issue and answer it, already, once and for all. Still, remnants of the old Scott, the cautious Scott, the man whose life had been predicated on obligation and a hyper work ethic that left little room for sentiment, kept him from giving his brother a straight answer.

He lowered his hand to hook it on his hip. "All I know is, I want Christina in my life in a way I've never even imagined wanting any woman before. And that if I let this opportunity slip through my fingers before I've explored every angle on how I could make it work, I'll regret it for the rest of my days. And I can't exactly explore those options in Atlanta." After several more beats passed, Scott asked, "You still there?"

"Yeah. I'm here. And you know what? You're right, we only get one shot at this. So if this is what you want, go for it. But, for all our sakes, don't wait much longer to tell the others."

"I won't. I promise."

He disconnected the call, then turned to find Wendy standing in her kitchen doorway, her eyebrows about to fly off her head.

"You're *staying?*"

"It would appear so."

"For *good?*"

"Sure hope so."

His baby sister gawked at him for several seconds, then, on a squeal of delight, waddled over to give him a huge hug.

After a rotten night's sleep, constantly interrupted by disturbing dreams involving Scott and her mother and being all tangled up in tornado debris that turned into a giant cobweb she couldn't break out of because her feet were encased in cement, Christina awoke with a start, scaring poor Gumbo half to death.

Then she remembered she had a checkup with the orthopedist that day and whimpered. Because how, exactly, was she supposed to pull that one off?

However, being an intrepid soul, she decided that since her broken foot actually felt more or less okay, and she drove with her other one, and here was this perfectly good car sitting right outside her front door, she'd drive her own dang self into San Antonio. What was the worst that could happen? The doctor would yell at her?

Except when, an hour later, Scott landed on her doorstep, she realized, no, *this* was the worst that could happen.

"Hey, boy," he said, squatting to roughhouse with the ecstatic dog, and Christina didn't know whether to scream or cry or laugh or what. "I didn't...I thought...after yesterday..." She stopped, grabbed a breath. And hopefully a coherent sentence. "Why are you here?"

"You have a doctor's appointment today, right?"

"Um, yeah. But I was going to drive myself there."

Scott looked up at her as if she'd said she'd just had breakfast with Elvis. "I don't think so." Then he rose, and before she could blink took her face in his hands and kissed her. Sweetly. Gently. But still like a man used to going after what he wanted. And getting it. And once again her spirit did that roller-coaster thing, soaring to what felt like the top of the world, only to drop right back down, leaving her dizzy and slightly woozy and unable to get her bearings.

"You don't play fair," she whispered, dropping her head to his chest.

"I never do." Then he tucked his fingers under her chin, lifting her face so their eyes met, and whispered, "Trust me."

Her eyes flooded. "Why would you even say that?"

"Because you need to know you can. Now let's get moving or you're going to be late."

Yeah, didn't take a brainiac to interpret that dream, did it?

"How was your visit with your mother?" Scott asked once they were on the road.

He would bring that up. "Short. And not exactly sweet."

"I'm sorry."

"So'm I." Then, because she was feeling ambushed and off balance and still light-headed from the kiss, she said, "She's convinced you're only interested in me for sex."

She could practically feel him flinch, followed by a short, startled laugh. "Excuse me?" When Christina shrugged, he tossed a frown her way. "Don't tell me you agree with her?"

"I don't know," she lied. "Are you?"

"No! Not to put too fine a point on it, but if that's what I was after, I would have hardly chosen a woman nursing a broken foot, now would I?"

"So…you don't have the hots for me?"

He got very quiet. "In case you missed it, I didn't exactly kiss you yesterday like I would have kissed my grandmother. But the implication that I—" He stopped, his jaw so tight she could've sharpened a knife on it. "I *care* about you. A great deal. But I know you're skittish, for reasons known only to you—"

"And what difference does it make, what those reasons are? Eventually, you'll go back home, and I'll fade into a vague memory—"

"Except I'm not."

"Not, what?"

"Going back."

Now it was her turn. "*Excuse* me?"

"You heard me." His eyes glanced off hers before he returned them to the road. "I've been scouting out ranch properties with a Realtor the past couple of days. And I think I've found the perfect place, right next to your field where the old barn was—"

"Wait, wait, wait…you're buying a ranch?"

"Yep."

"Here. In Red Rock."

"Since that's where you are, it seemed like a logical choice."

Silence stretched between them like the interminable country highway before Scott blew out a breath.

"And did that sound like stalker-speak as much to you as it did to me?" he asked.

"From anybody else it sure would."

He coughed into his hand, then said, "I meant what I said, about not giving up easily. Call me stubborn, or an idiot, but…I'd still like to see where this goes. Between us, I mean. And I can't do that from four states away. Besides, I always wanted to raise horses—remember my telling you how much I loved to ride when I was a kid?—but once I started working for my father I shoved that dream aside, thinking maybe after I retired…"

And on he went, like the world wasn't imploding around them. Or maybe his world wasn't, maybe his world really was finally landing right side up. Well, whoop-de-do for him—hers sure as heck wasn't. Her world had gone *kaplo-ooey,* like a hot dog cooked too long in the microwave.

Because how could she deny that, given her druthers, part of her wanted to see where this was going, too. Even if that part—which would be that tiny remnant still clinging to the fantasy—was at odds with the much larger part that knew exactly where this was going: nowhere. That no matter how many detours they took along the way, or how pleasant those detours might be, they'd still end up at the same place, wouldn't they?

Christina turned her face to the passenger-side window so he wouldn't see how hard she was fighting tears. *Damn* the man—her only safety net had been that he'd go home someday. But if he was staying...

Kaplooey.

"Does knowing how well your foot's healing make it feel better?"

Hanging on to Christina's crutches in case she needed them at some point, Scott leaned against the far wall of the hospital elevator, giving her the space she so obviously needed. Talk about feeling like a first-class dolt—she'd barely looked at or talked to him since his announcement. And here he'd prided himself on being an expert at finessing the client, knowing exactly when to take the next step in negotiations.

"Yes, actually," she said, giving him a meager smile.

Except Christina wasn't a client. Or a convenient, willing distraction from his work. He'd do well to remember that. Apologizing wasn't something that came naturally to him—he was his father's son, after all—but even he knew he'd blundered, big-time, by springing his news on her before she was ready.

He waited until they'd gotten out to his car in the parking lot before saying, "I'm sorry—"

"You threw me a curveball, Scott," she said quietly, then finally looked at him. "I honestly thought…" Shaking her head, she looked away.

"What?"

Her eyes met his again. "That you were flirting. Okay, that's not fair, considering everything you've done for me, but…" She heaved a sigh. "I guess I figured you were simply amusing yourself. That there was no way you could be serious."

"Why is it so difficult to believe that I am?"

"Ohmigosh—where would you like me to start? Like I said before, we're so different. And the way we met…honestly, meeting on *The Bachelor* would be more normal—!"

He cupped her face, watching the words snag in her throat, silently cursing at all that ambivalence in her eyes. "And I've been on more 'normal' first dates than I can count, 95 percent of which I couldn't wait to be over so I could get back to work. So tell me one thing, and be honest—no qualifiers, no prevarication, just the truth. Do you have feelings for me, too?"

Their gazes tangled for what seemed like an eternity until she finally said, "Yes. But—"

"Then I don't give a damn how we met, I'm only glad we did. Because you woke me up. Made me take a good, long look at myself and realize I didn't like what I saw. Who I'd become. If nothing *ever* happens between us I'll always be grateful for that."

He released her to lean against the car, his arms crossed. "Yeah, I stuck around because of you. I never denied it. But I'm staying because to go back to what I was before, *who* I was before, would be a lie. And every day I'm here the clearer that becomes."

After another exchanged look, she said, "My leg's getting tired, I need to sit."

Scott stepped aside so she could get into the car—under her own steam—shutting the door after her then going around to his side. By the time he got in, she'd clearly regrouped. "So you're saying no matter what I do you're still buying that ranch?"

He could almost feel the relief radiating from her. He started the car, backed out of the space. Finally, got it through his thick head that if he had any hope whatsoever of this working he'd have to let her call at least some of the shots. "Yup."

Christina lifted her hand to gently scrape the edge of her thumbnail across her bottom teeth, a habit she indulged when she was nervous, he'd noticed. Then she dropped her hand and he ventured, "Would you like to see it?"

A pause. "I thought it wasn't yours yet."

"I can't get into the house, but I can drive onto the land. The owner's not there."

After a moment she nodded. "Yeah. Okay. Why not?"

Even though it nearly killed him, Scott managed not to grin *too* hard.

She could have lied. Kept her traitorous feelings to herself. Except for one thing they'd already established—she was a sucky liar. And for another, she mused as Scott took her by the hand and leisurely led her across a vast pasture, she couldn't hide her emotions from him if her life depended on it. No man had ever given her the freedom to be herself as he had…or threatened her peace of mind more.

Good news, meet bad news.

"How big did you say the spread was again?"

"Not huge." His elbows now propped on the split-rail fence overlooking a pond edged in live oaks, Scott looked content in the way of a man who could pretty much make anything happen he wanted. "By Texas standards, anyway. Seven hundred acres and change. Close to a thousand if I can wrangle that adjacent parcel."

Christina laughed in spite of herself, even though she couldn't imagine owning that much land. Or any land, for that matter. "What on earth are you going to do with a thousand acres?"

"Anything I want?" And his being as nonchalant about buying an entire ranch as she might have been buying, oh, a carton of milk, only proved they were from different worlds. Why he couldn't see that—or refused to—she did not know. "Raise some horses. And kids. Watch those kids learn to ride."

She started. "So...how many kids are we talking?"

"Dunno. Two? Six? Haven't decided."

"Six?"

"Why not?" He nodded toward the house, a two-story, dormer-windowed jewel with a wraparound porch, set on a tree-crowded berm a half mile or so from where they stood. Late-afternoon sunshine gilded the white clapboards, the simple but stately columns. "House has seven bedrooms. May as well fill them."

"Because it would be inefficient otherwise?"

He glanced over, his grin doing very, very bad things to her stomach. If this was his way of backing off, she was in serious trouble. "That would be my take on it. House is barely five years old and impeccably decorated, by the way. And everything stays, down to the towels in the bathroom cupboards."

"Really? How come?"

"Owner passed away about a year ago. The widow's moving to California to be with their daughter, wants to

start completely over. So she's selling the house furnished."
He made a face. "Although I could do without the heads."

"Heads? Oh. As in, deer and such."

"As in. Will they let me stay in Texas if I don't hunt?"

"That could be an issue," she said, and he gave an ex-aggerated sigh, making her laugh. Making her regret... so much. Then he pointed to the west. "There's state-of-the-art stables for twenty horses, right on the other side of the house. Training arenas. Pastures for days." He paused. "And a kennel."

"A kennel?"

"She raised champion beagles. It would be perfect for—"

"Don't say it."

"—your doggy hotel."

Her throat got all tight. "You're doing it again."

"Taking your needs into consideration? Guilty as charged."

"Speaking of dogs," she said, before her imagination ran away from her. "I need to get back to mine."

"Sure thing," Scott said lightly, offering her his arm to walk back over the uneven ground to the car. He plugged his iPod into the car stereo and chose his classical playlist for the ride back to her place, the soothing music filling the space where conversation should have been. When he pulled up in front of her apartment, however, he said, "I have to leave for a few days. Will you be okay?"

"Of course. But why—?"

"I can't very well dump this on my father over the phone."

Steady though his voice might have been, even she could hear the faint anxiety edging his words. "Scott...if this is the right decision, it'll all work out exactly the way it's sup-posed to."

His eyes tilted to hers, the barest of smiles curving his lips. "Exactly what I keep telling myself," he said quietly, and too late she realized what she'd said. A second later he leaned over and touched his lips to hers, then kissed her forehead. And oh, my, was it hard to get out of the car, to watch him drive off, feeling like her heart was gonna pop out of her chest. At which point she finally, hopelessly admitted that all that kicking and screaming she'd been doing to not fall for the guy?

Had been one big, fat waste of time.

Chapter Nine

"Like hell you're moving to Red Rock," John Michael said, his voice lethally soft. A voice Scott recognized all too well. And had more than steeled himself against.

"I'm not sixteen anymore, Dad," Scott said, every bit as softly, his hands shoved into his pants pockets as he stood in front of his father's massive, curved black glass desk at FortuneSouth's headquarters. Through the floor-to-ceiling windows behind his father the entire Atlanta skyline seemed to glower at Scott in disapproval. "This is what I need to do—"

"Become a *rancher?* Have you lost your mind?"

"No, Dad. I've finally found it."

To his right, leaning against a wall of mahogany bookcases, his brother Mike released an incredulous laugh. "You've dedicated your whole life to FortuneSouth. You can't simply walk away on a whim. For crying out loud, Scott—what about *loyalty?*"

Scott's eyes swung to his brother's. "Considering the amount of business I've brought in? The untold number of fires I've put out over the last ten years? Somehow I think I proved my loyalty some time ago."

His brother looked genuinely perplexed. "Then why—?"

"Because I finally woke up and realized this isn't me." He faced his father again. "And why would you want me in a position of authority if my heart's not in it anymore? That's only a lose-lose situation for everybody, don't you think?"

As Mike muttered something Scott was frankly grateful he couldn't hear, he and his father stared each other down. Then John Michael lowered himself into his leather chair again, rubbing his mouth for a moment until he let his hand fall to squint at Scott. "I know what this is. It's some kind of post-traumatic reaction, from the tornado—"

"No, it's not. Yes, what I went through made me reassess my life, but trust me, I'm thinking perfectly clearly. More clearly than I ever have in my life—"

"You can't quit," his father blustered. "I won't hear of it. To leave me, to leave us, in the lurch like this…that's not the way I raised you."

"Then consider this my thirty days' notice," Scott said mildly. "Whatever duties I can't immediately assign to someone else I'll continue to handle from Red Rock. If nothing else, I can promise you a smooth transition. I owe you at least that much."

"You owe me a helluva lot more than that."

"No, Dad. I don't. Especially since you've made it more than clear that Mike's the heir apparent. Which is fine by me," he said, facing his brother again. "I'm done competing with you, big brother." At his brother's snort, Scott frowned. "What?"

"Can't *deal* with the competition anymore is more like it. That's what this is all about, isn't it? You've finally caved."

Scott laughed. Not what his brother expected, judging from the slightly startled look on his face. "Not at all. I did realize, however, what a waste of energy it is, fighting for something I *don't even want.*"

He caught the exchanged glance between his brother and father, fought the surge of irritation that neither was taking him seriously. "Don't give your notice yet, Scott," John Michael said. "Go on back to Red Rock, take all the time you need—"

"Dad. You're not listening. I'm not going to change my mind. When have you ever known me to make an impetuous decision?"

"Never. Which is why I know this is an aberration. That given enough time you'll realize what a damn fool idea this is and come to your senses—"

Mike's laugh brought both their heads around. "I can't believe I didn't see this sooner... Dad, don't you get it? It's about that gal from the airport, isn't it?" he said to Scott. "The one you stayed behind to 'help'?"

His father's gaze rocketed to his. "Is that true, Scott?"

Until things were settled with Christina, Scott had intended to leave her out of the equation. Especially since he knew his parents hadn't yet fully reconciled themselves to Wendy's precipitous marriage, their approval of Marcos notwithstanding. But at least Wendy's relocation to Red Rock hadn't left a gaping hole in the company's infrastructure, even if it had in his mother's heart. Now, however, he realized he did owe his father something even more than that smooth transition—he owed him the whole truth. Or as much of it as Scott himself knew.

"Yes," he said, over Mike's triumphant, "I knew it!"

"A...woman?" his father said, his expression even more

gobsmacked than before. "You're chucking it all for a *woman?*"

"Not just *a* woman, Dad. The woman I want to spend the rest of my life with." *If she'll have me.*

"So let me get this straight…you met somebody in Red Rock barely two weeks ago and you're ready to give up everything you've ever known, everything you've achieved, for her?"

"That about sums it up."

"Then…what was all that about wanting to be a rancher?"

Suddenly, Scott wanted nothing more than for his father to *understand,* to feel the scorching heat from inside Scott's belly that had rendered him willing to incur not only his father's disapproval, but his wrath—the exact opposite of everything he'd ever thought he'd wanted. Feeling like a Jimmy Stewart character, Scott grabbed the back of the chair in front of John Michael's desk and yanked it out, then dropped into it, pitching toward his father to snag his gaze.

"What keeps you going, Dad? What makes you glad to be alive?"

John Michael looked slightly taken aback. "Pride," he shot back after a moment. "In this business. In family—"

"Exactly. Now tell me why."

"I don't have time for this—"

"Of course you do. Answer the question."

A beat or two passed before his father said, "Because they're mine."

Scott fought a smile. "Then don't you wish the same for your children? To be able to take pride in their *own* accomplishments? To be their own people the way you've been?" He paused. "To have families of their own they can be proud of?"

"Then marry some girl right here in Atlanta. You could have your pick—"

"I don't want 'some girl' from here. I want Christina."

"Why?"

"Aside from her being the most genuine woman I've ever met? Or that she's not impressed with my investment portfolio? Not to mention I get this, this incredible *rush* every time I hear her laugh, or see her smile…" He paused, caught a breath. "I want this woman in my life because she's smart and funny and brings out the best—or at least what I hope is the best—in me without even realizing she's doing it. And because I know if I let her go, especially without putting everything I have into trying to make things work between us, I'll spend the *rest* of my life comparing every woman I meet to her."

Taking no small pleasure in his father's even more flummoxed expression, Scott leaned back in the chair, his hands loosely folded over his abs. "You know, you can be pissed at me all you want, but you have no one to blame but yourself."

"Me?"

"You. Because not only do we all carry your genes, but nobody has ever set a better example of how to go after what you want—and getting it—than you." He let the smile bloom. "Mom's told us it took you three years to convince her to marry you."

To Scott's great delight, color flooded his father's face. Then John Michael stood, linking his hands behind his back as he turned to the window and the vista beyond. "But the ranching thing—"

"Dad—from the first time I rode I've *always* wanted to be around horses, to be able to walk outside my front door and see nothing but land and sky. But to please you, I did my best to convince myself that what I wanted didn't matter. Or that it could at least wait. So tell me—in my place, would you have done the same thing?"

His father turned, the window's aura behind him obliterating his expression. "And this woman...she's really worth the risk?"

A sweet, soul-deep calm such as he'd never known settled over him. "Yes."

John Michael faced the window again. "I need some time to process all this."

"Take all the time you want," Scott echoed, getting to his feet. "As long as you keep in mind that I'm not changing mine."

Mike followed him through his father's outer office and into the black granite-walled, tenth-floor lobby fronting the elevator bank. Scott punched the down button, then stepped back, his eyes cutting to his brother's frowning profile. "Okay. Spit it out."

A moment passed before, a tight smile curving Mike's mouth, he angled his head toward Scott. "I don't think you have any idea how worthy an opponent you've been. How much knowing you were breathing down my neck kept my ass in check all these years. Hard as this is for me to admit, I wouldn't be nearly the asset to FortuneSouth I am if it hadn't been for you."

His turn to be poleaxed, apparently. "Thank you—"

"I'm not done yet." Sucking in a deep breath, Mike glanced toward the elevator door as it silently slid open. As the brothers entered the stainless steel-and-cherrywood-trimmed car, Mike punched the first-floor button and leaned back. "But I can honestly say I never really *admired* you." One corner of his mouth tilted up, he looked at Scott again. "Until today. Nobody knows better than I do the guts it takes to stand up to Dad. So whatever you do,

I'm behind you. A hundred percent. Because damn, bro…" Mike extended his hand. "You *rock*."

A moment passed before, laughing, Scott gripped his brother's hand. Now, he mused as he crossed through the glass atrium main lobby and through the middle of three massive revolving doors, the only obstacle left was winning over Christina.

Piece of cake, right?

With a loud, frustrated groan, Christina threw off her bedcovers and grabbed for the cast, strapping it on and clumping to the kitchenette to make herself some instant cocoa. From the end of the sofa, Gumbo heaved a great doggy sigh and slid to the floor, yawning as he plodded across the floor to sit catawhompus at her feet.

"I wasn't supposed to miss him, dammit!"

Gumbo wagged his head in slow motion, his big old ears flapping, followed by the *God, again?* eyeroll.

So she might have expressed the sentiment a time or six over the past couple of days. But if the turkey's plan had been to get her so used to having him around she'd feel downright lost when he wasn't, it was working.

Dammit.

The cocoa made, she clomped back to the living room and eased herself onto the sofa, the wind's melancholy moan outside doing nothing to boost her mood. Gumbo hopped up to lay his head on her lap, offering sympathy for about ten seconds before he passed out again.

Of course, she supposed there was always the possibility that, once back home, Scott would come to his senses and realize this whole thing with her and wanting to buy a whole *ranch,* for heaven's sake, had been about as real as Oz had been to Dorothy. Except she'd caught the look on his face when he'd shown her the property, like he'd seen heaven. So she was going to take that as a "no." Especially since Scott didn't strike her as the kind of man given to being fickle.

And every time he looked at her…oh, dear Lord, she got tingles thinking about it—

"No!" she said, loudly enough to wake the dog. Sensing her distress, Gumbo gave her a worried look and several slobbery kisses, doing his level best to make it better. On the table beside her, her phone buzzed—an incoming text. At two in the morning?

She snatched up her cell, getting all tingly again at the sight of Scott's picture, a stealth one she'd taken when they'd been at the ranch.

Pathetic, thy name is Christina.

Can't sleep. Missing u.

Christina stared at the message for the longest time. She didn't *have* to answer. Really. After all, it wasn't like he expected her to. Or anything.

U do realize, she typed, is middle of night?

Gumbo? That u?

See, it was stuff like that, that had her all balled up and confused and, okay, fine, wanting him so bad she could hardly see straight. The goofy stuff, the unexpected stuff. The stuff that made her laugh even as she rolled her eyes harder than the dog. Smirking, she texted back, Yeah. But, dang, is hard 2 txt w nose.

Seconds later the phone rang. With a mix of excitement and dread, she answered. "Hello—?"

"Oh. I was expecting Gumbo."

The grin popped out before she could catch it. "Oh, shoot, was he texting again? I really wish he wouldn't do that, I keep getting these random texts from some poodle named Snooki." So sue her, it was two-freaking-thirty in the morning.

"Ah," Scott said. "Too much eyeliner, enormous…" He paused. "Hair?"

"The very one, how'd you know?"

"I can smell the cheap perfume from here. Tell Gumbo he needs to watch out for those Jersey bitches—they'll eat him alive."

Christina burst out laughing. "That's *terrible*."

"But true. If he knows what's good for him, he'll stick with the local gals."

"Clearly your experience with Texas gals is limited."

"Also true," Scott said, the smile in his voice making her toes curl. "But a situation I look forward to remedying as soon as possible."

"Um…we're not talking about Gumbo's love life anymore, are we?"

"Nope."

Her face burning, she hauled herself to her feet and hobbled into the kitchen to rinse out her mug. "So…how'd it go with your dad?"

"You could at least try to be subtle."

"Subtle is for weenies. So?"

Scott sighed. "I said my piece, he fumed and ranted and refused to accept my resignation, but no blood was shed so I'm counting it a success. He's also convinced I'm out of my mind, of course, but then, so is everyone else."

"And that doesn't at least give you pause?"

"What everyone else thinks? Why should it? I'm done seeking other people's approval, Christina. And I cannot tell you how freeing that is. Which reminds me…my Realtor called, the owner accepted my offer, so we can go to closing next week."

Back in bed, she froze in the middle of tugging up the covers. "Oh. Wow. So…fast?"

"Great, huh? Anyway, I'm taking an extra day or two

here to tie up some loose ends, pack up my personal things from the condo, put the place on the market. But I have a surprise for you."

"O-oh?"

"You remember the resort we passed on the way home from the hospital? There's a gift certificate for you and a guest waiting at the front desk, for a full day of pampering."

"Scott...no. I mean, that's very sweet, but you've done so much for me already—"

"And I'm going to keep doing things for you, so deal. Get some sleep now, and I'll see you when I get back to Red Rock. Okay?"

"Okay," she said, heaving a great sigh as she set her phone on her nightstand. *Okay?* Not even remotely.

Which undoubtedly made her the most reluctant Cinderella in history.

"Frankly," Wendy said as she settled her enormous self into the chaise next to Christina's in the spa's luxurious sunroom, "I don't know whether to kiss you or my brother for thinking of this. I haven't been able to see my feet since November, let alone paint my toenails. So this is heaven."

At one with a chaise so comfortable Christina almost wouldn't have minded dying in it, she had to agree. Unlike Enid, who'd turned down Christina's invitation with an impassioned declaration that the very *idea* of people she didn't know from Eve touching her half-naked body was at the very least unseemly, if not downright repulsive. Not that Christina didn't have to fight the giggles while trying to select from the long list of scrub/wrap/massage options that sounded more like lunch than treatments. But once the skilled staff began their ministrations...ohmigosh, she was a goner within a minute flat.

Besides the massages—they even had special accommodations for Wendy's pregnant belly—they'd had facials and mani-pedis, although Christina had had to forgo the "pedi" part of that for obvious reasons. Now, wrapped in plush white robes, they lounged by the kidney-shaped indoor pool, shaded by a veritable forest of trees and shrubs happily thriving in the sunlight-flooded room. Lunch would follow, the magical day ending with Christina's first professional haircut in...years.

So maybe she could get used to this.

She settled back in the chair and closed her eyes, the gurgling of an unseen fountain mingling with Mozart or somebody in the background. "Marcos doesn't mind?"

Wendy had hinted that her husband had some issues with not being able to keep Wendy in the manner to which she was accustomed. Even though Wendy had assured him that having her own home and a husband who adored her far outweighed the frills she'd willingly given up.

"That he gets a very happy wife at the end of the day? Not a bit. So...I suppose you know Scott's found his ranch?"

So much for relaxed. Opening her eyes, Christina faced her new friend. "Yes. But tell me something, since you know him a lot better than I do—do you think he's making the right choice?"

"Why wouldn't he be?"

Christina looked down at her lap. "It seems so...fast."

Opening the neck of her robe a bit, Wendy sagged back in her chair and tossed Christina her trademark disarming smile. "It's the Fortune impulsive streak. Like our own personal fault lines, long overdue for some major shifting." The smile widened. "Except for me, who's been shifting constantly since I was born, much to my parents' dismay. I'm guessing Scott's has finally worked its way to the surface. You mark my words, though, the others will follow. And sooner rather than later, if my hunch is correct."

"I'm confused—so you do think Scott's being impulsive?"

"For once in his life, yes. But that's not a bad thing, considering that my siblings' usual modus operandi is to think everything to death before they make a decision, and then only if it's one guaranteed not to ruffle feathers. If you ask me, it's about time Scott—and everyone else—started thinking with their hearts. Doing what *feels* right instead of what they *think* is right."

"But what if that impulse *isn't* right? Because there's a lot to be said for thinking through something as important as changing your entire *life*."

"Oops." Scott's sister reached across the space dividing them and touched Christina's wrist. "This isn't about his buying the ranch, is it?"

"Oh, Wendy…" Her forehead pinched, Christina met Wendy's amused gaze. She wanted to believe in new beginnings, in taking chances, she really did. But for every thought that came, encouraging her forward, ten more rushed in to remind her of the risks. "What on earth does he see in me? We have virtually nothing in common—"

"Neither do Marcos and I. On the surface. And yet I've never felt this comfortable with anyone in my whole life. Christina…this may be a stretch, but I'm going to guess my brother sees what I see—besides the whole cute-as-all-get-out thing you've got going, I mean. That you're fun to be with and bighearted and *good* with a capital *G*. If you've got those basics down, the rest will follow."

"Meaning he sees me as a diamond in the rough."

"No, I meant that if those core values mesh, nothing else means squat." Wendy frowned. "Do you really think Scott sees you as someone he can mold into whatever image he wants you to be?"

"It had occurred to me."

"That's not Scott, Christina. And if that's what he'd wanted, believe me, there were *plenty* of women only too willing to turn themselves inside out to please him."

"And that's supposed to make me feel better?"

"Yes. It is. Because he didn't want any of them. He wants you. Exactly as you are."

"So you're saying I should cancel the hair appointment?"

Wendy laughed. "No way. We always have the right to re-create our *own* image." Then she sobered. "Look, it's not my place to tell you what to do, or what you should think. But I love my brother, and it's pretty clear he's very, very serious about you. If you feel the same way, then why not simply roll with it?"

With that, Wendy leaned back and closed her eyes as if it was all solved, leaving Christina to think, *Why not, indeed?*

Chapter Ten

With a jolt that sent a renewed thrill of anticipation through him, Scott's commercial flight touched down in San Antonio, on a clear, mild day that hinted of spring. Marcos met him at the airport, looking marginally more relaxed than the last time Scott had seen him. Then again, that could be sheer exhaustion.

"Hate to ask...but how are things going?" he asked as he shouldered his carry-on bag and fell in step with Marcos through the concourse.

"Javier's still hanging in there, the restaurant's still standing and your sister and I are still married," Wendy's husband said with a tired smile. "So I'm counting my blessings. But since we're already in the city, do you mind if we swing by the hospital?"

Scott checked his watch. "I'm closing on the ranch at four, so that's two hours yet. Plenty of time."

"Then it's a done deal?"

"All but the signing. And the check."

Grinning, Marcos clapped him lightly on the back. "I'm glad. And Wendy will be beside herself. She doesn't complain—too much—but I know she misses her family."

They arrived at the hospital twenty minutes later, running into Dr. Cuthbert, the neurologist Dr. Rhodes had praised so highly, as she emerged from Javier's room. The tall, graying brunette shook hands with Marcos before steering them back to the nurses' station.

"I just got off the phone with your father. But I'll tell you what I told him, that Javier's making enough progress to start bringing him out of the coma within a week or so. And no," she said, her expression kind, "we have no idea what to expect. How, exactly, the brain works remains very much a mystery, and every patient's experience is different. He may well be disoriented at first, or even angry that he can't remember what happened. This is going to require great patience on everyone's part."

Marcos nodded, then pushed out a breath. "And…his legs?"

"His orthopedist can explain everything in more detail, but from what we can tell the broken bones are healing very well. But there was a lot of muscle damage, and Javier will have been immobile for nearly a month." The doctor paused. "He may have to relearn how to walk."

When Marcos softly swore, Scott frowned at the doctor. "Dr. Rhodes said your rehab facility is good?"

"A lot better than good, Mr. Fortune. One of the best in the country. In fact…Leah?" She called out to a slender young woman in bright blue scrubs chugging past, her long auburn hair caught back in a ponytail. She turned, pale brows lifted in a makeup-free face. "I'd like to introduce you to Leah Roberts, the rehab nurse who'll most likely be assigned to Javier's case. Leah, this is Javier's brother, Marcos. And Marcos's brother-in-law, Scott Fortune."

"Oh!" Closing the space between them, Leah tucked her clipboard under her arm to shake Marcos's hand, then Scott's, her grip firm and confident. As was her smile. "I saw your brother earlier today," she said to Marcos. "Along with the rest of his team. We've been discussing various options for his rehabilitation once he's brought out of the coma."

"How long...?"

Leah clasped the clipboard to her chest. "That will depend on your brother," she said gently. "But he's got youth and health in his favor." Then her smile flashed into a full-out grin. "Not to mention an enormous support system, from what all the nurses up here tell me. That counts for a great deal." Her pager buzzed. "Shoot, I'm so sorry," she said, apology flooding her hazel eyes as she backed away to punch the elevator button. "I'm already late for my next appointment. But they've got your number on file, right? So I'm sure we'll be in touch."

The doctor made her excuses as well, leaving Scott and Marcos free to see Javier. Thanks to an MP3 player with speakers, classical guitar music greeted them when they entered—one of Javier's favorite musical genres, Scott already knew. Although the obligatory heart and blood pressure monitors were doing their thing, as well as the ever-present IV, for all intents and purposes Javier simply looked asleep, if thinner than Scott remembered.

"Hey, man," Marcos said softly, twining his fingers around his brother's and launching into a funny, upbeat monologue about something that had happened in the restaurant the other day. As heavily as his brother's condition must have been weighing on the younger man's heart, clearly he was determined not to let it show.

When Marcos said, "Scott Fortune's here, he wants to say hi," Scott stepped closer to the bed. Picking up on the obvious cue, Scott told Javier about his decision to move to Red Rock, the ranch that would soon be his, how much he was looking forward to being a real part of the community.

Once back on the road to Red Rock, Marcos glanced over Scott with a half smile. "Thanks. For talking to Javier like that."

"No problem."

"Not for you, maybe. For other people…they forget that just because he can't outwardly respond, it doesn't mean he's not aware. Nobody knows how much he's taking in, obviously, but Dr. Cuthbert told us how important it is to keep the atmosphere positive, to not talk negatively about him when we're in the room, or act like he's not even there. And that sensory stimulation helps—the music, touching, reading to him, even favorite smells. It all helps keep him connected. We hope, anyway."

"I'm sure it does."

They chatted about Scott's plans for the ranch for the rest of the ride, until they pulled into Marcos's driveway alongside Wendy's car. Having finally turned in the rental when he flew back to Atlanta, Scott followed his brother-in-law into his house long enough to dump his bag, give Wendy a hug and ask if he could borrow the prized vintage Mustang she'd had driven out to Texas.

"Keys are in my purse. I take it everything went okay with Dad?" she said, slowly following him back to the front door.

"As well as could be expected." The keys retrieved, he bent over to give her a quick kiss on the top of her head. "And I promise to tell you all about it later."

Her arms like chicken wings as she supported her lower back, Wendy grinned. "Don't hurry back on my account."

"Wasn't planning on it," he said, her laughter following him all the way out to her car.

He might have said, "Hi." Maybe even, "I'm back." Christina didn't remember. Or care, frankly.

Not that she'd planned on locking lips with the man the second she opened her door. Nor was she sure who had launched him/herself at whom. But now, ten, fifteen seconds into the kiss, all she knew was she could no more *not* have kissed him right then than she could have flown.

Although come to think of it, she was flying pretty darn high right now, wasn't she?

Their mouths still joined, she vaguely heard the slam of her front door as Scott kicked it shut, Gumbo's whine of concern, then her back was against the wall, her hands held over her head as Scott sweetly assaulted her mouth with more passion—and talent, it should be noted—than she'd ever experienced. And her entire body egged her on, as well as her heart, scurrying along behind and whispering, *Me, too, me, too, me, too.*

Or maybe her heart was in the lead, it was kinda hard to tell what with all the sighing and gasping and the idiot dog hopping around as if he wanted to get in on the act.

Finally Scott backed away and looked at her. And smiled. And her heart whispered, *Would I lie to you?*

Just like the serpent chatting with Eve, yep.

But Scott was fingering her hair and grinning like nobody's business, and thinking was kinda not her top priority, right at the moment. "I like it," he said, and she clicked in enough to remember she'd more or less given the stylist at the spa free rein.

Christina combed one hand through the shorter, highlighted layers feathering around her neck and shoulders, the weightless bangs which made her eyes look enormous, exactly as the stylist had promised. "Good thing, since you paid for it."

"But do *you* like it?"

"Me? I love it."

"Then that's all that matters." He kissed her again, light and breezy, then grabbed her hand, dangling a set of keys in front of her with the other.

House keys.

"It's yours?"

"Every square inch of it." Scott's hand found her waist, tugging her close. "How 'bout a tour?"

Anticipation sizzled in the pit of her stomach. And not only about seeing the house, she thought as the sizzle meandered to points north and south and pretty much everywhere in between. And you know what? Maybe it was time to give in to the sizzle. To simply enjoy the moment. Because for darn sure she didn't have a whole lot of moments like these.

Sorry, Mama, she thought, even though she wasn't.

"I suppose I could fit it into my schedule."

Scott kissed her nose. Then her lips. Then, briefly, her neck. Right under her earlobe. Yeah. There. "I hoped you might. C'mon, boy—"

"Um…how's about we leave the dog home this time?"

Scott's eyes swung to hers, dark and curious, like those of a man wondering if he'd heard right. "You sure?"

"Very," she said.

Even though she wasn't at all.

"Good Lord," Christina said when they finally wound up back in the spacious, slate-floored family room off the cook's paradise of a kitchen. "You need a GPS system just to find a bathroom!" Her brow furrowed, she glanced up at the enormous buck's head mounted over the stone fireplace, shuddered, then clomped to one of the two leather sofas facing each other and collapsed into it.

"So what do you think?" Scott grabbed a suede pillow off the other end to cushion her foot when she lifted it onto the square, also Texas-sized, inlaid coffee table between the sofas, then sat beside her, plunking his feet up on the table, too.

On what sounded like a weary laugh, she faced him, her newly lightened hair fanning over the caramel-colored leather behind her head. The woman looked better in jeans and a hooded sweatshirt than most women sporting a thousand bucks' worth of designer fashion. No lie.

"It's real pretty and all, but criminy, Scott—this room alone is twice the size of my whole apartment. I do realize you're used to living in places a bit bigger than that, but doesn't this feel a little…over the top? Even for you?"

His arms crossed over his chest, Scott contemplated his Italian loafers for several seconds. "For one person, you mean?" he said at last.

"Well, yeah. Unless you're plannin' on having the horses live in here with you."

Laughing, he unfolded his arms to slip one behind Christina's shoulders and pull her close. She didn't resist. "One thing you need to know about me—I never do, or buy, anything without considering its investment potential." Massaging her shoulder through the soft fabric, he laid his cheek on her head. "How much something will increase in value over the years."

"You mean…like if you wanted to sell it at some point down the road?"

"In some cases, yes. But not in this one."

She lifted her eyes. "I don't understa—"

He caught her mouth with his, a little "Yes!" sounding in his brain—and other places—when she immediately softened, opening to him, her tongue meeting his in a playful dance that he found exceptionally...encouraging. But when he broke the kiss, her eyes still searched his, rife with questions.

"This is an investment in my future," he said softly, stroking her cheek. "And I hope...an investment in ours."

"Ours. As in...you and me?"

"And Gumbo, if he's up for it."

"Don't make jokes, Scott, don't..." She pulled out of his arms, floundering about in an attempt to get up.

"I'm dead serious, Christina. I always have been. And if you don't believe me—" he fumbled a bit himself, pulling the ring box out of his shirt pocket "—believe this."

She gawked at the aqua velvet box in his hand as though it were about to blow up in her face, then turned the gawking on him. "You *are* insane."

And it probably was crazy, to make this kind of commitment, this soon. Even crazier to ask her for one. But his entire life he'd deferred to logic, to common sense and reason and doing things the "right" way and none of them had ever made him feel one-tenth of what he felt when he looked into Christina's eyes. So he flipped open the box, anyway, to reveal the ring, a modest emerald-cut sapphire flanked with diamond baguettes.

"You said you liked blue," he said.

"Oh, for pity's sake," she said, laughing a little, and he felt the anxiety unfist inside him.

Her smile faded, though, as she shook her head. "You'd really put your heart on the line like that for me?"

Scott glanced down at the ring, still in his hand. "I think I already have." When she hmmphed out another soft laugh, he said, "Look...if you're not ready to think of

this as an engagement ring, then don't. I completely understand. But I couldn't think of another way to show you I'm
not flirting, I'm not teasing…and for damn sure I don't see
you as some sort of 'project.' I want to share this house, my
life, with you. I *love* you," he said softly into her I-don't-
believe-I'm-hearing-this eyes. "And I promise I'll wait as
long as it takes to close the deal."

On a cross between a huff and a groan, Christina finally
got to her feet and stiffly walked to the picture window
overlooking the sweeping lawn and one of the ponds
beyond. "Is that what I am to you? A deal?"

Yearning bled through her words, gave the lie to her
defensive posture. Scott came up behind her to wrap her
up in his arms. "The best damn deal I've ever run across,"
he whispered into her ear, feeling her rapid pulse compete
with his. "And the only one I've ever truly cared whether
I landed or not."

Gently, he twisted her around to face him, his fingers
winnowing through her hair to cradle the back of her neck,
their mouths so close he could feel her breath, coming in
short, sweet bursts. "And if you can't trust your intuition,
trust mine. Because it's never been wrong yet."

Never in her life had she wanted to believe so badly. To
let herself fall into the promise in those warm brown eyes.
If this is a dream, Christina thought, *I don't want to wake
up. Ever.*

But nobody knew better than she did that wanting wasn't
enough to change what was. And that trusting had gotten
her into trouble before. In other words, eventually she'd
wake up. And so would Scott, she wagered.

Only, when she did, she didn't want it to be one of those
frustrating dreams that comes to a screeching halt right

before the good stuff happens. And anyway, if she initiated it, she was in control, right?

So she stood on tiptoe to kiss him, deep and open-mouthed and with what she hoped was clear intent, melding her body with his until she felt his unmistakable response against her belly, dimly remembered sensation though that was.

His hands found their way to her shoulders, gently setting her apart as hope and caution tumbled in his eyes. "Just so we're clear...?"

Christina blew out a breath. "You want to talk deals? Here's mine. I want to make love to you so badly I can barely think straight." When his brows shot up, she added, "But it has to be on my terms. Meaning...no promises. And I know that's not fair to you—"

"Why don't you let me be the judge of that?" he said with a lopsided grin, slipping his hands around her waist and yanking her so close you couldn't've slipped a credit card between them. Then he kissed her again, all slow and sweet, at which point she realized that staying in control was a pipe dream. He swept her into his arms and carted her off upstairs into the master bedroom, all done up in shades of green, or maybe blues—she wasn't exactly focused on the décor at the moment—and set her on the bed.

"Don't look up," he said, and of course she did, to find a great horned animal of some sort looming over the bed. "Told you not to look," Scott said when she shrieked out a laugh, then lowered her eyes to discover he was nekkid.

She couldn't move. Or speak, barely. Although she did manage to get out, "I don't know how frisky I can be, with this foot."

And he said, "Not to worry, I can be frisky enough for the two of us."

wasn't just whistling Dixie. Whew.

Grinning, he started to undress her. Like he wasn't in any hurry, certain evidence to the contrary. She felt like... like a much-looked-forward-to present being carefully unwrapped, a thought that made her giggle and brought tears to her eyes at the same time. And when, after what felt like hours, there was nothing left between them but heated glances and dry-mouthed anticipation, he got down to serious business.

How is it I've lived without this? she idly wondered as Scott patiently—and, apparently, with no small delight—stoked fires she'd thought long gone cold, only to realize what she'd had before? No comparison. Still, she was in control, in charge, nothing was happening without her permission, her consent—

"Let go, sweetheart," Scott commanded, thrilling her, even as she thought, on a gasp, *Let go? Completely? Not on your life,* a moment before she arched and tensed and screamed—wasn't like anybody could hear her...and then—*then!*—he made her scream again.

"I didn't know I could do that," she got out when her breathing finally slowed and her brain cells came out from hiding.

"I did," Scott said, and then started up all over again with the kissing and the stroking and the feathery touches in—oh, sweet heaven!—exactly the right places until her eyes damn near crossed, and the phrase *putty in his hands* came to mind before he levered himself over her, capturing her gaze in his as if he could see right through to the other side. "How's the foot?"

She sputtered a laugh. "What foot?"

He reached for a condom—and where had that come from, pray?—but she shook her head, kicking the sadness to the curb. "Not necessary, I'm safe." Then she smiled. "You?"

He stroked her bangs off her forehead. "You trust me that much?"

And oh, dear Lord, did she. About this, anyway. "Yes. I do." Then before she could shift underneath him, lift her good leg, he did it for her, sliding inside her, his gaze still welded to hers as he took charge. Took over.

And there wasn't a damn thing she could do about it. Or, frankly, wanted to, at that moment, the surrender too sweet, too heady. Until she linked her hands at the back of his neck and snaked her good leg around him, to hold him still when he tried to move.

"Not yet," she whispered, her eyes closed. "I want to remember this forever."

Chuckling, Scott nuzzled her neck and every nerve ending she possessed sighed with bliss. Traitors. "Not sure about forever, but I can maybe give you thirty seconds."

"Deal," she said, opening her eyes to nearly choke on the desire and hope and trust she saw in his. Once again, the fire kindled, and she caught her lip between her teeth as the first wave rolled through.

And kept on going.

This is getting to be a habit, she thought as she floated back to earth in time to catch Scott's liftoff, and she twined her arms around him and held on tight.

As if he were actually hers.

Afterwards, he settled between her legs, his head on her chest where she could toy with his dark, rumpled hair as the regrets already began to show their smarmy little faces, taunting her for yielding the one thing she'd promised herself she wouldn't.

And she didn't mean her body.

At her sigh, Scott lifted himself up enough to meet her gaze again, his brow puckered as he knuckled away the single, lazy tear dribbling down her cheek. "Hmm. Not the reaction I was going for."

She frowned back at him. "You made love to me."

"Um...yeah. Kinda thought that was the point."

"No, I mean..." With a shaky laugh, she touched his cheek. "You made love to *me*. Put me first. Nobody..." Her eyes filling again, she shook her head.

Scott shifted to hold her close, tucking her head underneath his chin. "You're welcome," he said, and she burbled a laugh. Then he said, "Don't move"—as if she could—and got out of bed, grabbing a throw from a nearby chair to wrap around his waist before he left the room. A minute later he was back.

With the ring.

Seated on the edge of the mattress, he twisted the ring so the stones flashed in the afternoon sunlight. "You want forever?"

You have no idea, Christina thought sadly as she tugged the sheet up over her breasts. But how could she possibly trust what she knew absolutely nothing about? And yet she felt powerless to resist when Scott took her hand into his, slipped the ring on her finger. "It's a promise of my commitment. Not yours. But every time you look at this I want you to remember, as close as we just were?" He smiled. "It's only the beginning. Because I will always be here for you, honey. I swear."

Staring at the ring, she felt her face burn. She needed to come clean. Now. While there was still a chance of getting out of this without anyone getting hurt.

"Scott, I—"

"If you don't like it, you can pick something else out that suits you better."

"No, I love it, it's just—"

From somewhere on the floor, his phone rang.

"You should probably get that."

"That's what voice mail is for. You were saying?"

"Get it," she said, forcing a smile as she pushed him aside to get up. "I'm going to go take a quick shower, anyway," she said, gathering her clothes. "I'll be back in a jif."

Shaking, she closed the bathroom door behind her, crossing her arm over her breasts to watch the pretty little ring wink in the lights bordering the giant framed mirror. She could almost hear it chiding her, for being at the very least dishonest. For letting Scott believe he could make her into something she'd never be.

She stretched out her hand, her blurred vision softening the sparkle.

But not the ache in her heart.

By the time Scott dug his phone out of his pants pocket, he'd missed his father's call. John Michael's message was typically brusque. *"Call me."*

Talk about an afterglow killer.

Although truthfully, Scott thought as he ducked into another of the four upstairs bathrooms to take his own shower, there was nothing his father, or anyone else, could say or do to derail how good he felt right now. A feeling that went way beyond that relaxed state that came with sexual release. Because while Scott was no stranger to sex, this was the first time he could say he'd *made love*.

And man, was that an eye-opening experience, or what?

For Christina, too, he thought on a chuckle as the hot water pummeled his back, if all those startled gasps were any indication, the mind-blowing yin yang of her asserting, then yielding control. Never had a power struggle been so much fun.

Except…it was driving him nuts, that he had no idea

how to banish the uncertainty still fighting for purchase in her eyes. That had sent her scurrying away, clearly not wanting company in the shower. Judging from what they'd just shared, he highly doubted he was pressuring her into something she didn't want. Desperately, if his intuition was correct.

So why, he wondered as he headed back to the bedroom, a towel wrapped around his hips, did she still look so damn afraid to trust him?

Afraid of *him?*

His mood now soured, he returned his father's call, putting the phone on speaker mode as he buttoned his shirt.

"Hey, Dad—what's up?"

"Brad Stevens called, wondered why you haven't been in touch with him."

Scott pulled in a deep, silent breath through his nose. "Because I turned that account over to Mike. Which I explained to Brad when I spoke with him yesterday."

"But he likes *you.*"

"And I'm flattered. Really. But he's not my client anymore. He's Mike's. By the way, you and Mom are going to love my new house. Seven bedrooms, everyone can stay here when they come out after Wendy's baby arrives. Christina says the hunting trophies have to go, though, they creep her out—"

"You already bought her a house?"

Slightly taken aback, Scott paused in the midst of buckling his belt. "I bought myself a house. Which, yes, I want Christina to share with me—"

"Dammit, Scott—I cannot believe you're chucking it all for some snack bar waitress!"

Never, not once, had his father ever struck any of them. But his words now stung with all the force of an actual blow. Then he frowned.

"Who told you she was a waitress?"

"It doesn't matter. Why? Isn't she?"

"No. I mean, she was, yes—as a means to put herself through school, for heaven's sake. Which for one thing is hardly a crime against humanity and for another doesn't even begin to define who she is. You're many things, Dad, but I've never known you to be a snob. Mom was your attorney's receptionist, for crying out loud—"

"The summer we met, yes. Between her junior and senior year at Smith. The woman's after your money, Scott—can't you see that?"

Furious, Scott snatched up his phone from the dresser and put it back on private…the precise moment he glanced into the mirror to see Christina behind him in the open doorway. The eyes met for barely a second before she wheeled on her casted foot and clomped away.

"I've got to go, Dad," Scott muttered as he went after her, pocketing his phone before his father could reply.

"Christina, stop!"

Since it wasn't like she could exactly run down the curved staircase, she halted at the top, one hand clutching the wooden bannister. "Please don't say that sounded worse than it was. And don't touch me!"

She sensed Scott take a step back. Sensed, too, that he was not a happy camper right now. "Yeah, that was pretty bad. I'm also sure it's a knee-jerk reaction, because I'm resigning, moving away. He's upset, but he'll get over it. Besides, it's what I think about you that matters, not what my father thinks—"

"He called me a gold digger!" she said, wheeling on him, the déjà vu making her dizzy. "Or as good as. How on earth could we possibly have a relationship when your father clearly hates me?"

"He doesn't even know you—"

"Didn't stop him from judging me, did it? And I told you not to touch me!" she said when he grabbed her shoulders and yanked her to his chest.

"Tough," Scott said into her hair. "Look, I'm none too pleased with him, either, at the moment. But please believe me—" He relaxed his hold to set her back, his gaze caressing hers. "Whatever you heard, it's highly uncharacteristic. When he does get to know you, he'll love you as much as I do—"

His phone buzzed. "See, that's probably Dad right now, calling back to apologize...oh." Frowning, he brought up the text message, then looked at Christina, all the color drained from his face.

"That was Wendy. She's in labor. And she can't get hold of Marcos."

Chapter Eleven

Twenty minutes later they pulled into Wendy's driveway, the worry tensing Scott's face twisting Christina inside out. There'd been no time to get her home first, which seemed to bother Scott a lot more than it did Christina, who'd switched into crisis mode the moment she'd heard.

"Wen?" he called out the instant they were through the door. "Where are you, sweetheart?"

"In our b-bedroom!"

Scott roared down the short hallway, Christina right behind him. Wendy was lying on her left side on top of the covers, her arm protectively curled around her bulging middle.

"There was some sort of supply crisis at the restaurant," she whispered. "M-Marcos had to make a quick trip up to New Braunfels, I wasn't doing this when he l-left! And I didn't call him right away because I thought it was gas or something at first—"

"Shh, shh, shh…" Scott sat on the edge of the bed, stroking her hair away from her tear-streaked face and making a lump rise in Christina's throat. "Did you call your doctor?"

"What d-do you think? S-she said to d-drink a couple g-glasses of water and lie on m-my left side to see if the c-contractions stopped. It's been more almost an hour and they h-haven't."

Scott stood. "What's her number? We can meet her at the hospital."

"It's on the refrigerator. But she said—"

"I don't give a damn what she said. I'm not about to take any chances with you. Or my niece. And I'll call Marcos while I'm at it. He can meet us there, too."

After Scott left in search of the number, Christina awkwardly lowered herself to her knees to fold her hand around the young woman's, willing herself to stay in the moment. To not give in to the fear. The memories. Wendy gave her a shaky sigh.

"I'm glad you're here."

Christina returned her smile. "Me, too. Did your water break?"

"N-no."

"Then this is probably just a very scary false alarm—"

"Ohmigosh!" Turning over Christina's left hand, Wendy's eyes flashed to hers. "What's this? Did Scott *propose?*"

Damn. With everything else going on, she'd forgotten about the ring. "It's…no. Not quite." Christina shoved her hair behind her ear and tried to remove her hand from Wendy's viselike grip. "It's more like…a promise ring."

Wendy angled Christina's hand to get a better look. If nothing else, at least it distracted Wendy from her own plight. "That must've been some promise."

You have no idea, Christina thought as Scott returned. "Okay, it would be quicker for me to get you there than to wait for the EMTs, so let's get cracking. Do you have a bag or something?"

"It's so early I hadn't p-packed one yet…oh!"

At her scrunched face—although more in fear than pain, Christina surmised—Scott scooped his sister into his arms, only to let out a curse. "Crap—I can't take you in the Mustang!"

"There's a minivan in your neighbor's driveway," Christina said, hustling out of the room as fast as the stupid cast would let her. "Maybe they'll let us borrow it!"

The pleasant, middle-aged woman who answered the door was more than happy to oblige, handing over the keys before her husband could even lever himself off the recliner behind her.

"Oh, my goodness, that sweet girl! You tell her Morton and me'll keep her in our prayers, you hear?"

"Got 'em!" she called to Scott seconds later, who swiftly carted Wendy across the yard, gently settling her into the van's middle seat. A minute later, they were off.

"Hurry," Wendy whispered behind them.

"You got it, honey," Scott said, gunning the poor minivan probably faster than it had ever gone before.

Scott dropped into the waiting room chair, exhausted but still tingling from the previous hour's excitement. Marcos had gotten there not five minutes after they did, the same time as Wendy's doctor. After her exam Wendy had been admitted and was being given medication to stop the labor. If it took, she could probably go back home tomorrow, although she'd be on strict bed rest for the rest of the pregnancy—no muffin baking!—which ought to make his always-on-the-go sister even more nuts.

If it didn't, he thought with an anxious spasm, Dr. Curtiss assured him they had an excellent neonatal unit, that MaryAnne would get the best care possible.

Returning from the ladies' room, Christina sat beside him, her makeup-free face pale in the ghastly artificial light. Scott reached for her hand, holding on tight in an attempt to pick up where they'd left off when Wendy's frantic text had come through.

Her eyes briefly cut to his before, blushing, she looked down to brush nonexistent lint off her lap. "They're going to be fine, Scott."

He frowned slightly, wondering if she'd deliberately misinterpreted the gesture. Then he exhaled. "Wendy was a preemie, too. Six weeks early. Scared us all half to death."

"I can imagine," Christina said after a moment. "Then again, she certainly didn't seem to suffer any ill effects from it, right?"

One side of his mouth tilted. "Physically, no. Although there's a reason she was spoiled to death."

"I don't think she's spoiled at all."

"You didn't know her back then. Whatever she wanted, she got. Or made everyone miserable until she did." He looked over; Christina's eyes were still lowered. "You did good back there. Keeping Wendy from losing it. Not to mention me."

Slipping her hand out of his, she sort of laughed. "Oh, yeah, I'm just a regular rock," she said, twisting the ring around and around on her finger, like Gumbo trying to make himself comfortable on his bed. "Long as it's somebody else's drama."

"Hey. You okay?" When she lifted bewildered eyes to his, he said, "We kind of left things...unfinished. Back at the house."

"Oh. Right." Her nostrils flared when she blew out a breath. "It's not that. Well, not entirely. It's…being here. It brings back memories."

"From after the tornado?"

"No. From—"

"She's asleep," Marcos said, coming up behind them and sinking into the chair catty-corner to Christina, the lingering concern in his eyes duking it out with the relief evident in his relaxed posture. "So far the meds seem to be working, she hasn't had a contraction for an hour. But she's already three centimeters dilated and 50 percent effaced, which the doctor said is unusual for a first-timer this early in pregnancy."

"So…what does that mean?" Scott asked.

"That they're going to keep her for a few days instead of sending her back home tomorrow. Just to be sure." Then he gave them a weary smile. "Thanks for everything, but you guys don't have to stick around."

"She's my sister, believe me I don't mind—"

"I know you don't," Marcos said, getting to his feet. "But hopefully she's going to stay asleep for a while now and keep that baby inside. So please. Go."

Scott stood as well, holding out a hand to help Christina up. "You call me, though, if anything changes?"

"You got it."

However, he waited until they were in the van and out of the hospital parking lot before he said, "So what were you saying before Marcos showed up? About being in the hospital bringing up memories?"

Her gaze fixed straight ahead, Christina forked her fingers through her bangs, then folded her hands in her lap, and for a moment Scott thought she was going to clam up again. Before he could call her on it, however, she said, very quietly, "Seven years ago, I was in that maternity wing. Only, that time, there was nothing anybody could do."

Scott's breath caught in his throat. "You lost a baby?"

"I wasn't as far along as Wendy. Only four months. But, yes."

"Damn, honey…being around Wendy—"

"And you can stop that right now. For one thing, you didn't know. And for another, it's not like I can avoid pregnant women for the rest of my life. Besides, I've always believed God puts us where He needs us to be. And that we don't always get a vote in the matter. This wasn't about me, it was about Wendy and MaryAnne."

"Well, now it *is* about you." Scott's hands tightened around the steering wheel. "Why didn't you tell me about the baby?"

"For what it's worth, I was going to earlier, only Wendy called and somehow that didn't seem like the right time for a stroll down memory lane."

"When has it ever been?"

He sensed her eyes cut to his profile, then back to the taillights a hundred feet in front of them. "You said it didn't matter."

"As to how I feel about you? No. But it's obviously coloring how you feel about me." He gave her a brief, hard look. "In which case, yeah. It matters. Because whether you want to admit it or not…it's holding you back."

"I know," she whispered, then sighed out a breathy laugh. "It's like…my head's that closet crammed to the gills with all that stuff you simply do not want to deal with. Which is kinda funny, when I think about it, considering how much I detest clutter of any kind…"

She did that raking her thumbnail across her bottom teeth thing for a moment…then, with a sigh, finally yanked open that closet door.

* * *

They'd been high school sweethearts from their sophomore year on, she said quietly, steadily, as Scott drove, focusing on the headlights piercing the darkness in front of them. Chris and Chris, joined at the hip, homecoming king and queen. The perfect couple who never had a single fight.

Even though he came from money and she didn't.

"Not that it made a lick of difference to us," Christina said as a sick knowing-where-this-was-going feeling shuddered through Scott. "Or so I'd convinced myself—but his folks weren't exactly thrilled. Especially since Christopher was their only child, and they had Big Plans for him. Which did not include little ol' me. So I guess we had that whole Romeo and Juliet thing going on. Although that story didn't end too well, either, did it?"

Scott hesitated, then said, "Since you're still here, I take it there was no poison involved?"

"Not the kind you drink, no. But thoughts can be a kind of poison, too. Even if it takes a long time to take effect. In any case, right after graduation we eloped, because it was rebellious and romantic and proved we were adults who could make our own decisions. Only then he brought me home—his home, I mean—as his wife and all hell broke loose."

"I take it his folks didn't come around?"

Her laugh sounded raw. "You might say. His father pointed at me like I was a stray dog who'd followed Chris home and said, 'You're old enough to marry that piece of white trash, then you're damn well old enough to pay your own bills.'"

"Crap," Scott said softly, realizing. "Then my father—"

"Yeah, that was definitely one of those déjà vu things. At the time, however, I was still caught up in the dream and determined to make it work. We were both working crappy jobs, but the plan was he'd go to college and get his degree, then I could get mine. Except..." She paused. "Except then I got pregnant. And Chris freaked. Told me no way could we deal with a baby right then, that I had to get...to get rid of it. And...I told him I would."

"Damn, honey..."

"Oh, I had no intention of going through with it. But I would've said almost anything to get him to stop yelling at me. To buy me some time. Lord, Scott, I was scared out of my gourd. Yeah, he'd begun to snap at me now and then, but I chalked it up to his being tired all the time. That night, though...it was pretty bad. But by that point, I *couldn't* give up. Couldn't let on I was in over my head, that my mother had been right all along—"

"About what?"

"That I had no business being with somebody like him. That he'd get tired of me eventually, realize he'd made a mistake. Same as my daddy had done, apparently. Because, you see, he'd come from money, too. So the last thing I wanted was to hear her *I told you so.* Not that I had clue one what I was going to do, but I guess I hoped once the shock wore off Chris would adjust to the idea. Because we were a *team,* right? As we had always been. Only..."

Crossing her arms, she snorted. "Here's what I didn't realize until much later—while I was all about the romance, apparently Chris's primary goal was to piss off his parents. So he married me." She shrugged. "Why it never occurred to him they'd cut him off, I do not know. But they did. And...I guess he felt pretty trapped."

Scott glanced at her. "By what? And please don't say 'me.'"

"By circumstances, then."

"Of his own making."

"True, but…we did have some good times, Scott. I swear. A lot of good times."

"As long as things were easy?"

Her shoulders bumped again. "As long as he got his way. Then again, maybe I was expecting too much of him—"

"Don't defend him, Christina. Or make excuses. He was your *husband,* for crying out loud."

Several beats passed before she said, "In theory, yes." A long breath hissed from her lungs. "In any case, suddenly I was four months gone, no closer to knowing what I was going to do than I had been when that little plus sign showed itself…right about the time Chris pulled his head out of his butt long enough to realize my body was changing. We had another fight. A big one. He grabbed his keys and stormed out of our second-floor apartment, yelling that that I'd broken my promise and that he should've listened to his parents, should've…" She shook her head, her hand fisting in her lap. "I ran after him. But my heel caught on one of the steps and I fell."

Even though he already knew the outcome, Scott felt his heart turn over. "And Chris?"

Christina tucked her hair behind her ear. "To give him some credit, when I screamed he turned back, looking scared out of his wits. He called 911, stayed with me the whole time. And even though I was devastated about the baby, I truly thought he'd had his come-to-Jesus moment, that we'd be fine.

"But we weren't. Not by a long shot. He refused to let me talk about my feelings, acting like it'd never happened…" She shook her head, then sighed. "Eventually I had to admit that our relationship had miscarried long before the baby. Especially since…since I realized I couldn't stay married to somebody I no longer respected. And I h-hated him for what he'd asked me to do."

Scott's jaw hurt from the effort to not say what he was really thinking, what he'd be sorely tempted to do if the little weasel ever crossed his path. Instead he said, "Why wouldn't you?" and she shrugged again.

"We got a no-fault divorce a few months later. At least, it was called no-fault."

"It sure wasn't yours."

"I didn't shoulder the entire blame, of course not. But…" They pulled up in front of her apartment, but she didn't seem in any hurry to get out of the car. Instead, she shifted enough to face him, her forehead pinched.

"My mother and I have issues aplenty, God knows, but in this case she was right. I *should* have known better. Heck, I've always prided myself on being a realist, even as a kid. But I was so, I don't know…flattered, I suppose, when Chris picked me. Out of all the girls in school. *Me.* He seemed so confident. So in charge. Like he could make anything he wanted to happen. And it wiped common sense clean out of my head. Because when the chips were down we were obviously looking at life through different lenses. And all the wanting in the world for things to be different wasn't going to change that."

Dread swamped him even before she started to twist the ring off her finger.

"Christina—"

"I can't accept this, Scott. No matter how much I want to, or how much I love you. And I do love you, you've gotta believe that. But that doesn't change the fact that you and I, we look at life through different lenses, too. We can't help it," she said when he started to protest, "it's just the way things are. So, here—"

"Honey…you're tired and shaken because of what happened with Wendy—"

"Dammit, Scott—listen to me! Even if I didn't believe,

with all my heart, that we're not suited for each other... you know that vision you had of filling all those bedrooms with little Fortunes?" She grabbed his hand and pressed the ring into his palm, closing his fingers around it so hard the stones cut into his flesh. "I can't make that happen for you. Because the miscarriage, somehow it messed me up inside and I can't have b-babies. That had been my only shot. And it was selfish of me to sleep with you, to let you put the ring on my finger, when I knew I could never help you realize that part of your dream—"

On a sob, she shouldered open the door and clumsily got out, leaving Scott feeling like the wind had been knocked out of him.

But only for a moment.

She was still blindly fumbling for her keys in her purse when Scott pulled her into his arms, holding on so tight she could barely breathe.

"Let me go, dammit!"

He released her immediately, only to clamp hold of her upper arms, fury thrashing in his eyes.

Christina lowered hers. "I'm sorry I made you mad—"

"Oh, I'm way past mad, honey. You say you love me, but you have so little faith in me that you couldn't share what's probably the most important thing about you—?"

"That I can't have kids?"

"No! That you're in pain! And why on earth do you think you have to lug that pain around all by yourself?"

"Because maybe it's no one's concern but mine."

"Well, you're wrong. Dead wrong." He let his hands drop to stuff them in his jacket pockets, but his jaw was still rigid. "Independence is all well and good, it's one of the things I admire about you. But if I've learned nothing else in business it's that nobody accomplishes squat by themselves—"

"And maybe I do! Maybe I'm the exception to your rule!"

"Nobody is the exception to that rule. Nobody. Did you even tell your mother about the baby?"

"Oh, God, no," she said on a bitter laugh.

"Why not?"

"Because she would've only said the same thing Chris did, that it was just as well I'd lost it...that I wasn't any more ready than she'd been to have a kid."

"You don't know that for sure—"

"Enough to know I wasn't up for taking that chance. Scott, you're still not getting it. You can argue your point until you're blue in the face, but you can't *make* this work anymore than I can. Because nothing you can say changes the simple truth that *I don't know how to do this!*"

"Do *what,* for God's sake?"

"Let myself be loved! Be part of a healthy relationship! Whatever you want to call it. Because nobody, and I mean *nobody,* has ever stuck around long enough for me to figure it out." Tears streamed down her cheeks; furious, she swatted them away. "Being alone...it's safe. And after what I went through, I'm all about being safe. Although heaven knows you came closer than anybody to breaking through those barriers. Criminy, you're the first man I've slept with since my divorce. What does that tell you?"

His trembling grin would be her undoing. "That I should be honored as hell?"

"Nice try. But how about...it's like part of me is broken and I don't know how to fix it—"

Scott grabbed her shoulders again, gently shaking her. "And maybe you don't have to fix it yourself, dammit!

That's what *you're* not getting! Or don't you believe my feelings for you are real?"

"Of course I do!" she said to his tortured gaze. "But… but I still can't wrap my head around how it would work between us in the long run, any more than it did between Chris and me—"

"Sorry, honey, but that dog don't hunt. It never did, at least not from my perspective. Sweetheart—you and Chris were *kids*. We're not. *I'm* not. And in an adult relationship, both partners—*partners*—work on that relationship together. Work out the *problems* together. Children…"

Closing his eyes, he let his head drop back, like he was asking for guidance, then looked at her again. "My heart breaks for you because you can't have them. For *you*. Not me. Because I know," he said, palming his chest, "I'd love a child we adopted every bit as much as I'd love one you gave birth to. I *love* you. And I've never said that to another woman. How's that for a confession?"

Her heart shattering, Christina touched that beautiful face. "I hear everything you're saying, I really do. But…I can't help it—this all still feels like something out of a storybook. And I don't dare trust it, no matter how much I want to. Especially since…"

Turning, she shakily got her key in the lock, not facing him again until the door was open and Gumbo rushed outside. The only creature, she realized, whose love she did trust. And how sorry was that?

"You know, I used to wonder, once the Prince married Cinderella? If he looked at her one day and realized…they really had nothing to talk about."

Scott looked at her for a long moment, then said quietly, "This isn't about trusting the fairy tale. Or even me. It's about trusting yourself. What *you* want. What you *deserve*. And it pisses me off to no end that for someone so determined not to let circumstances define her…that's exactly what you're doing."

Then he stalked back to the car and got in, slamming his door so hard it set off the Jetta's alarm.

Chapter Twelve

Scott was still in a slamming and banging mood when he got back to Wendy's, although he took care not to show his irritation when he returned the minivan's keys to the neighbors, giving them a brief rundown on what had happened. Minutes later he was on the couch, his phone in one hand, his head in the other as he waited for Blake to pick up. Although he agreed with Wendy that it was probably best not to tell their parents about her condition, at least for the moment, Blake would skin him alive if he discovered they'd deliberately kept him out of the loop.

And calling his brother would divert Scott's overwrought brain from dwelling on what was going on with Christina. Or would have, had not Blake's voice mail picked up the call instead of the man himself.

Annoyed, Scott left a curt message, then stood, ramming the phone into his pocket and heading back outside before he suffocated in the tiny house. Granted, part of him was inclined to cut his losses and walk away. Unfortunately, the stubborn part—which would be the part that grabbed a project by the throat, refusing to let go until he'd seen it through—wasn't onboard with that idea.

At. All.

Especially since the…resignation in her voice, which only intensified the deeper she got into the story, make him abso-freaking-lutely crazy. Maybe it wasn't up to him, he thought as he found himself walking toward Main Street, to fix her, to eradicate her pain…and maybe it was. Because what if God or whatever *had* put him in that part of the airport for a reason, and that reason was to save—for a lack of a better word—Christina?

Or for her to save him, which was a far more likely scenario.

Whichever it was, how could he turn his back on that?

Sure, he'd been momentarily blindsided by her bombshell that she couldn't have children. But, come on, he hadn't even considered having kids a month ago. So pretty stupid to allow it to derail him now—

His phone buzzed.

"Hey, guy," Blake said. "What's up?"

"Wendy's in the hospital," Scott said as he walked. "She went into early labor."

"Holy crap, Scott, is she okay?"

"Yeah, yeah, she's fine. They got it stopped, but they're keeping her for a few days to make sure it doesn't start up again. But the plan is to let her come home, as long as she stays in bed."

"For more than a *month?*"

"Three weeks, at least. If she goes into labor then, she'll be far enough along that the baby won't be considered premature."

"Wow. Who's going to take care of her?"

"Now that you mention it, I have no idea. Marcos's time is already splintered between the restaurant and seeing to Javier—"

"I'll do it. Come out there to help out, I mean."

Scott laughed. "You? Wait on the Princess?"

"She adores me. It'll be good, I promise. I'll simply work from there. Did you get the ranch?"

Instantly, visions flashed, of Christina gawking in astonishment at the huge kitchen…the late-afternoon light haloing her blond hair as she stood in front of the family room window…of her sweet cries as she shattered beneath him—

"Yeah. It's mine. Plenty of room if you'd rather stay there instead of Wendy's."

"And…Christina?" At Scott's dry laugh, Blake asked, "What's going on?"

"Damned if I know."

"Dude."

"Let me clarify that. She's told me plenty, enough to figure out there's a lot of past garbage cluttering up her head. Then, as if that's not bad enough…" He sighed. "She overheard Dad basically accuse of her being after my money."

"Ouch."

"Yeah. Even though that couldn't be further from the truth."

"You sure?"

"Positive. As positive as she is that I'm going to wake up one day and realize I've made a mistake."

After too long a pause, Blake said, "You sure you won't?"

"I'm not infatuated, if that's what you're asking. And no, this isn't about the thrill of the chase, either. And, sorry, obviously I didn't call to bitch about my love life."

"Good. Then we can talk about mine."

"Wasn't aware you had one."

"Har, har. But, as you said, that staring death in the face thing really does have a way of making a person reassess his life. Choices he's made, opportunities that slipped through his fingers."

"Such as...?"

"Brittany."

Scott's scalp prickled. "Blake...no—"

"Gorgeous gal like her...why is she still single? I'll tell you why—because we left things hanging. You remember that fundraiser we attended in the fall? How she and I 'just happened' to keep running into each other? Maybe the timing was off before, but now...it's fate, I tell you. And this time I intend to give fate a helping hand—"

"And there's nothing more pathetic than a man trying to win back his old college girlfriend. Give it up, guy. Let the past stay in the past—"

"No can do, bro. And I have you to thank for the inspiration. Now all I have to do is formulate a plan—"

Scott grimaced.

"—and you—don't you dare give up. You want this woman, you fight for her, you hear me? And I'll let you know tomorrow when I'm coming in."

Pocketing his phone, Scott ambled past the hodge-podge of architectural styles that made up the little residential street, frowning so hard his head hurt. Because while Blake was clearly off his rocker for wanting to resurrect a dead relationship, giving up on one that hadn't even gotten off the ground yet was something else entirely. But Christina was right, too, that this was one thing he couldn't *make* happen—

He stopped dead in his tracks as large chunks of their last conversation replayed in his brain, and with them, an idea. A crazy, long-shot idea that could seriously blow up in his face. But if he wanted to be Christina's prince, it would appear he had some dragon slaying to do.

He once more dug out his phone, scanned his Contacts, hit Send. She answered on the first ring, her already familiar cackle making him smile. "Yeah, figured I'd hear from you sooner or later..."

Scott had debated whether to call first or simply show up, finally deciding that, while the element of surprise often proved useful in business dealings, it could backfire in personal ones. Not the best way, perhaps, to establish a relationship with his potential mother-in-law. So he'd called.

Clearly nervous, Sandra invited Scott into the kitchen of the modest ranch house in the middle-class Houston suburb, where she offered him coffee and a slice of boxed Danish, both of which he refused.

"Your husband's at work, I presume?"

The woman's mouth tightened before she carefully closed the Danish box, then slid it toward the backsplash. "He's not here, no. Well. I suppose we may as well go and sit down..."

The living room was simply and inoffensively furnished, the only spot of color a bright orange, long-haired cat sprawled across the back of a gray-and-beige-striped sofa.

"Have a seat—"

"I'd rather stand, thank you," Scott said, pulling an old trick of his father's out of his arsenal and using his height to his advantage. Not to intimidate, exactly, but definitely to keep the upper hand in the proceedings.

Christina's mother briefly frowned, then shrugged, the gesture eerily reminiscent of her daughter's. In fact, beneath the trying-too-hard makeup, the defensiveness stiffening her shoulders—not that Scott could blame her for that, he supposed—he caught a glimpse of the same vulnerability as well.

Something else, God forgive him, that could possibly prove useful.

"Suit yourself," she said, sitting on the sofa. The cat immediately left his perch to settle on her lap. "I'm assuming Christina sent you?"

"No. She doesn't know I'm here."

"Then how'd—?"

"Doesn't matter. Mrs. Hastings—"

"Sandra, please," she said, apparently regaining her composure. "I haven't used that name in years."

"Fine. Sandra. Quite simply, I'm here because I love your daughter. Very much. And I want to marry her."

Despite an obvious attempt at keeping her expression blank, agitation bloomed in eyes more gray than blue. "And, what? You want my blessing?"

"Right now I'm more about getting answers. Because something's keeping her from saying yes."

The agitation yielded, barely, to a tight, yet almost triumphant smile. "How about…maybe she doesn't *want* to marry you? Nothing I can do about—"

"I don't think that's true." Scott shoved aside the front of his leather jacket to slip his hands into his pockets. "In fact, I know it's not. This isn't about what she does or doesn't want, but what she's believes she can't have—"

"And if, after all this time, everything I've been telling her has finally taken root? Then hallelujah. And frankly," Sandra said, gently pushing the cat off her lap to get to her feet, "I don't think you and I have anything more to discuss—"

"What's taken root," Scott said, blocking her way when

she sidestepped the coffee table on her way to the front door, "is fear. Fear that I have very good reason to believe you planted—"

"So what if I did? After everything that happened—"

"And what 'everything' would that be? Chris turning out to be a loser? Or her father walking out on *you?*" When Sandra's chin jerked up, Scott blew out a sigh. "Yeah, crap happens. People screw you over. So because of that she should never be happy again?"

She scooped the mewing cat off the coffee table, clutching him to her chest. "You rich men, you love to put ideas in girls' heads. Make them believe they're somebody they're not. Until you get bored with your little game and then…you leave. And you know what the worst part of it is? That you've shown 'em a world nicer than anything they've ever known, letting 'em play in it for a while, only to yank it away when you go. Do you have any idea what that's like, Mr. Fortune? To wake up and realize…it was all a dream?"

And there they were, the daughter's words echoed in the mother's. And, Scott could now see, the pain. Sandra's not wanting her daughter to suffer as she had—and she had clearly suffered, of that he had no doubt—was understandable. But he also suspected there was something else at work here. What, he wasn't sure. What he did know, however, was that the bogeyman was finally out of hiding.

Or at least showing his face.

"For whatever you and Christina have gone through," he said gently, "I'm truly sorry. I know you've both been hurt. But having money doesn't make me a bastard, Sandra. At least, I hope not. And I have never toyed with a woman's feelings in my life, or ever made a promise I wasn't absolutely sure I'd keep. So I'd hardly do that to someone who means everything to me. And make no mistake, your daughter has become the most important thing in my life."

Several seconds passed before Sandra stepped around him and continued to the front door, which she opened. Taking his cue, Scott joined her, where she laid one hand on his arm, the defiance mostly gone from her eyes.

"If I don't tell my daughter to be careful, who will? Because no matter what you think, I love her—"

"Then you might want to rethink how you show it."

Her hand popped off his arm as though she'd been stung. "You've got no right to say that to me."

"Your daughter's happiness is at stake, Sandra. If not her entire future. And I'll damn well say whatever it takes to make you realize that."

He started through the door, then turned, zipping up his jacket against the suddenly stiff breeze. "Nothing would thrill me more than to help Christina turn her dreams into reality. *Her* dreams, not mine. She'll also never want for anything. Not only for the moment, for the rest of her life. But far more than either of those, I can give her the one thing she's apparently had in pretty short supply, which is my pledge to love her as long as I live. Now I ask you… what mother wouldn't want that for her child?"

When she didn't answer, Scott let himself out of the house, praying more than he ever had in his life that his words had hit home.

Chapter Thirteen

It hadn't been the best couple of days she'd ever had, but Christina had always prided herself on being able to function, no matter what. Being productive instead of moping in front of *Judge Judy* and stuffing her face with Doritos. Or raw cookie dough. Which they now said could kill you, anyway. So she washed her hair and cleaned her house, tackled a few course assignments and tutored a couple of kids. Even took Gumbo for a slow, but steady, walk up to the 7-Eleven and back. Ogled the hunks who'd mysteriously appeared to get the pool up and running again. Like she didn't know who was behind that, even though Enid was playing coy.

She even took the Jetta for a spin. Of course she sobbed her lungs out when she got back, but still. It was something she needed to do.

Of course, if she'd thought all that activity was somehow going to keep her from thinking about Scott, and the hash she'd made of things, she was dead wrong.

It made no sense—she'd been perfectly okay before he'd blown into her life. Not only did she enjoy being alone, she cherished it. And she supposed she'd cherish it again, someday. When she was sixty, maybe. Or somebody invented a drug or machine or something that wiped out memories, so she'd stop thinking about that afternoon in his house.

Because she ached. Oh, dear Lord, she ached.

Sighing heavily, she finally gave up reading the excruciatingly boring text for her marketing class and got up from the kitchen table to go stand at her living room window, if for no other reason than to look at something besides the same four walls. It'd been cloudy and windy all afternoon, threatening rain and rendering the view even more dreary than usual. Unbidden, she thought of the views from Scott's ranch…the house…that bedroom…

"For pity's sake," she muttered, grinding her fingertips into her forehead like she could rub away the thoughts. "Cut it out!"

But still the memories jeered, sending tears streaming down her cheeks. She'd really, truly believed she'd loved Chris, that he'd loved her, had suffered mightily when it all fell apart between them. Compared with what she felt for Scott, however…

Like comparing "Chopsticks" to a Beethoven symphony.

Christina knew he thought she was Looney Tunes, that he didn't fully understand why she had to reject his offer. His love. But being in that house…it only proved what she'd been saying all along—that she wasn't enough for him. Heck, she wasn't even enough for the *house*. For herself, yes. Even for some other man, at least in theory. Because it would always be so…one-sided, wouldn't it? Scott had so much to offer her, but what did she have to offer him in return? And how soon would that be used up—?

"Oh, hell," she muttered, her thoughts scattering like roaches when she saw her mother's car pull up, wondering what truly terrible things she'd done in a past life to deserve this.

Christina watched helplessly as Sandra got out of the car, glared at the roiling clouds, then marched toward the front door, which Christina had opened by the time her mother hit the porch.

"Oh!" Sandra's hand flew to her chest. "You startled me!"

"Wasn't exactly expecting you, either."

"Is it…okay if I come in?"

"Um…of course." From where he lay beside the heating vent, Gumbo lifted his head, took in the situation, decided it wasn't worth his time or energy to investigate and flopped back down again.

"Can I get you anything?" Christina asked as her mother removed the same red wool three-quarter-length coat she'd had for years.

"No, I'm fine. And listen to you, acting like I'm a church lady paying a call." She looked…subdued, Christina thought. Less makeup, smaller hair. Like she'd lost some weight, judging from the way her hostess dress—a black sheath, adorned with a print scarf—hung on her frame. She carefully lowered herself to the edge of the sofa, her hands on her knees. "Your young man came to see me," she said, and Christina nearly fell over.

"Scott?"

"You got more than one?"

"No." Although she didn't exactly have that one, either. "Why?"

"I'm still not entirely sure, to tell you the truth. Although…" Sandra stretched out her fingers, then covered her left hand with her right. "He says he asked you to marry him."

"Not in so many words, but…he gave me a ring, yes. I didn't keep it."

Her mother frowned. "How come?"

"Because it didn't feel right. *I* didn't feel right."

"You're sure? I mean, it was entirely your decision?"

"Well, yes." Wondering what the heck was going on, Christina slowly sat on the ratty old recliner. "What's this all about?"

"He seems pretty convinced I had something to do with it. That I've…unduly influenced you. Or something."

"Oh. Well…you haven't exactly been encouraging—"

"Because I couldn't bear for you to go through again what you did with Chris." She reached up to fidget with the Hermès knockoff. "Like I did with your daddy when he left us high and dry, without hardly two quarters to rub together."

Color flooded her mother's pale cheeks as she leaned forward, becoming more and more agitated. "You and I, we're cut from the same cloth, you know? Attracted to the same kind of man. Only it never works out, does it? Not for me, and not for you. So I had to make sure you wouldn't make the same mistake, didn't I? To *protect* you, baby. That's all. That Scott Fortune…don't you believe all his pretty talk, Christina, you hear me? Because he can promise you the moon and stars and everything in between, but that doesn't mean he'll deliver. You know that, right? That we're both better off alone than having our hearts broken again by some rich SOB who thinks he can toss us away like old garbage—"

At that, Sandra burst into tears.

Tears Christina realized weren't for her.

"Ohmigod…" She looked at her mother as though seeing her for the first time. "This isn't about protecting me at all, is it? Which should come as no surprise since you never really have. This is about not wanting me to be happy because you never were!"

A tissue plucked from the box on the table beside the sofa, Sandra gaped at Christina. "What an awful thing to say!"

"But it's true!" Bolting to her feet, Christina clamped one hand to her mouth as one by one, the pieces fell into place. "Because it's always, always been about you!" When her mother pulled a face, Christina shook her head. "Was this supposed to be some sort of *pact* between us? That if you were miserable I was supposed to be, too?"

Her mother seemed to crumple in front of her. "Do you have *any* idea how I felt when you and Christopher started going together?" she whined. "That after everything that'd happened you took up with a *rich boy?*"

"And what did that have to do with you?"

Fresh tears leaked from her eyes. "I felt like I'd been betrayed!"

Christina wheeled around and crossed to the window, her arms tightly folded over her middle. "And you wonder why we don't get along."

After a long silence, her mother said, "No, I don't."

Frowning, Christina faced her again. "Come again?"

Her mother blew her nose again, then gave her head a little shake before lifting her gaze to Christina's. "Even then, I suppose I knew what I was thinking was wrong, even if I didn't know how to fix it. But the green-eyed monster had me by the throat so bad I couldn't think straight. And it only got worse, after you two got married. I was so lonely. And mad. At your daddy, at myself…" Her sigh was shaky. "And I was so busy wallowing in the mad and the hurt it never occurred to me there might be something past it."

"So, what? You cheered when my marriage fell apart?"

"No, of course not. I'm not that far gone. But..." She pressed her lips together. "But I guess I did feel vindicated, somehow."

"And you're still holding on to all this crazy, even though you're remarried?"

On a humorless laugh, Sandra stretched out what Christina realized with a start was her ringless left hand. "Harry left me," she whispered. "Two days after New Year's."

Christina bit her lip, feeling all those years of bitterness and frustration and anger dissolve in the face of her mother's obvious, and genuine, misery. The woman looked absolutely defeated.

"Oh, Mama...I'm so sorry." And she truly was. For so many reasons. "But why didn't you say something when you were here?"

"I was ashamed, okay? Didn't want to admit I'd messed up again."

Despite everything, sympathy tugged at Christina's heart. "It takes two to mess up, Mama."

But Sandra didn't appear to have heard her. "I was barely holding it together as it was, and then I saw you and Scott together that day, saw the way he looked at you, and that monster reared its ugly head all over again. I'm sorry, too, baby," she whispered. "More than I can say. If I think about it for more than five seconds, of course I want you to be happy. And much as it pains me to say this...I think Scott might be the one to do that for you. Because for sure I never saw in Chris's eyes, or your daddy's, what I saw in Scott's. B-but is it so wrong for me to be h-happy, too?"

And if she truly believed the Good Lord put people where He needed them to be...

Sighing, Christina sat beside her mother and took her hand. The woman grabbed on like she'd drown if she let go. Which Christina supposed wasn't that far from the truth. "Of course it isn't. But you need to talk to somebody. A professional, I mean. You've got some heavy-duty issues to work through."

"Like I can afford a therapist—"

"We'll work it out. I promise," she said. "Maybe we can find one of those two-for-one deals on Groupon or something."

Sandra pushed out a soft laugh. "You're probably right. But I have no idea where to even begin…"

"I'll take care of it." Not that she had any idea where to begin, either, but the prospect of venturing into hitherto-unexplored territory didn't hold nearly the terror for her that it obviously did for her mother.

Um, hello? Are you listening to yourself?

Christina sucked in a quick breath at the promise behind that revelation. She could practically feel her thoughts shifting, realigning themselves in her brain. Letting in the light. Holy cow—nobody had ever done for her what Scott had. Taken that kind of risk…for her. Put his butt on the line… *for her.*

But first things first. Like tending to the relationship in front of her, whether she wanted to or not. Except…she did, she supposed. After all, it wasn't like she could trade out this mother for a new one.

Besides, as tempting as it was to hold on to the bad feelings, not only had they not proved all that useful, when you got right down to it, but Christina knew it had also taken guts for her mother to show up here. Even if her original intent had been to cover her own patoot, the truth had worked its way to the surface anyway, hadn't it? So now maybe they could both work on healing.

"Mama? Do you suppose we could, I don't know. Start over?"

Sandra blew her nose. "You think that's even possible?"

"I have no idea. But I'm willing to try. If you are."

"Then...I think I'd like that. Very much."

"Okay, then." Her hands knotted on her knees, Christina shut her eyes, took a deep breath, then said, "I never told you why Chris and I broke up."

"I assumed it was because the two of you weren't suited."

"That's certainly part of it. But not all," she said over the rapidly rising lump in her throat. "I got pregnant."

"Pregnant? But..." When Christina's eyes flooded, her mother let out a soft moan. "Oh, honey...come here."

And she wrapped her arms around her daughter and stroked her hair as she cried, like it was the most natural thing in the world.

So they started talking. And kept talking, and sometimes crying, not only long into the night, but well into the next day—after Christina spent the rest of the night wide awake, praying her little heart out. So it was the middle of the afternoon, after Sandra finally headed back to Houston, before Christina brought up Scott's cell number into her phone, holding her breath for a moment before hitting Send.

"I need to talk to you," she said when he answered.

"Christina?"

"You were expecting Gumbo?"

After that soft, caressing, sending-shivers-up-her-back chuckle, he said, "I'm at the ranch. Out by the stables. Where are you?"

"On my way."

"I'll wait."

At the entrance to the long drive leading to the property, Christina pulled the Jetta onto the soft, weed-choked shoulder. Gumbo wriggled between the seats to nose her arm; she smiled down at that goofy face fixed so steadily on hers while the rest of his body shimmied. Then, looking back out the windshield, she sighed.

"Do I dare to do this?"

Still wagging, Gumbo cocked his head, the skin all pleated between his ears. Then he barked—it did take him a while to process information—and stretched his neck to give her forearm a slurpy kiss.

Admitting she was wrong meant chucking everything she'd believed about herself for more than five years...a burden she was only too glad to jettison. And small potatoes compared with what Scott had chucked for *her*. On another sigh, she started driving down the dirt road toward the house, rolling her eyes at the sight of the big-ass pickup parked in the driveway. It suited him, though, substantial but not flashy. Sort of a pewter color. Dignified. At least, as dignified as a truck the size of a small house could be.

She pulled up alongside it and got out, shielding her eyes from the sun as she and the dog walked—well, she walked, Gumbo bounced—around the house toward the stables. As she approached, a horse's whinny caught her attention. Her gaze veered to the right, to a magnificent black beast with a jagged white blaze, clearly entranced by whatever Scott was saying to him as he stroked the horse's neck. And oh, my, if he didn't look almost like a real horseman in his jeans and boots and black shirt underneath a denim jacket, and Christina's breath caught in her throat as she finally gave her heart its head, letting her love for this man flood her very being until it became so vast, so...*all,* it simply, finally, completely obliterated the fear.

Home, she thought, the single word as comforting as an angel's kiss—

"Gumbo, no!" she called when he made a beeline for the animal—dumb cluck probably thought the horse was a big dog. But when he reached the fence, he stood on his hind paws to brace his front ones on the middle rail, and the horse slowly lowered his head, making soft whuffing noises as he inspected this silly, stubby creature with the big ears and no sense whatsoever. Then he seemed to nod as if in approval before cantering across the paddock to the other side, tossing his shiny black mane.

"Took you long enough," Scott said softly, and she thought, *You ain't whistling Dixie, Bucko.*

Scott's chest constricted at how beautiful she was, the breeze messing with her hair, her long skirt gently molding to her thighs as she walked toward him.

"He's gorgeous," she said when she got close enough for Scott to hear her, to see the smile in her eyes a moment before he reached for her waist and pulled her in for a kiss. And she tugged him even closer and gave him everything she had. Everything he wanted. At least, as much as she could, he imagined, considering they were out in the open.

"So're you," Scott whispered, brushing her hair out of her eyes and making her blush.

"You don't seem all that surprised I'm here."

"You did call."

"No, I meant—"

"I know what you meant. And what I am, is damn happy."

She kissed him again, then pulled free to fold her arms across the top of the fence. But not as she might have before—nervously, in retreat. If anything she seemed completely at ease.

Content.

"When did you get him?" she said as the horse calmly plodded back over to check her out, too. Scott dug in his pocket for a piece of apple, which he handed to her. She held it out to the horse flat-palmed, giggling a little when his lips tickled.

"Yesterday. One of my cousins here told me about this couple who rescues abused horses and rehabilitates them."

When the horse softly nibbled her shoulder, Christina laughed and rubbed his velvety nose. "He's a rescue?"

"Yep. He'd lived the life of Riley before his original owner died. Kids sold him to some jerk who mistreated him. Animal control took him away about a year ago. Guy I bought him from said it took months to get Blackie to trust him—"

"Blackie?"

"Minute they told me his name, I knew he was mine." When she laughed, he mimicked her position. "I missed you."

"I could tell," she said, grinning. But focused on the horse. "How's Wendy?"

"You're stalling."

"You could say that. Well?"

The breeze shifted, cocooning him in her scent. He inhaled deeply, then said, "Coming home tomorrow. Blake's flying out to help take care of her before poor Marcos loses his mind. Between trying to keep on top of things at the restaurant and going back and forth to see Javier, he's already pretty fried. The last thing he needs is to worry about my sister, too."

Her cheek resting on her folded arms, she looked up at him. "And how is Javier?"

"They've started to bring him out of the coma. It's a

slow process, I gather. And once he's conscious…" He
sighed. "We just don't know."

Nodding, Christina stepped away from the fence, holding out her hand. Scott took it, giving it a slight squeeze
before leading her toward the house and up onto the porch,
gilded in the late-afternoon sun. The white porch swing
complained a little when they sat on it, laughing, but it held,
and when Scott wrapped one arm around her shoulders and
pulled her close, and when she leaned into him with a sigh,
he knew what bliss was for the first time in his life.

Then Gumbo scrambled up the stairs to join them, his
nails clicking against the floorboards as he trotted from
chair to chair, sniffing, tail wagging the entire time, until
he collapsed with a great sigh in a splotch of sunlight at
their feet, and Scott chuckled.

Christina smiled up at him. "What?"

"Just thinking how crazy I am about that dumb little
dog. Not quite as crazy as I am about his mistress, but
close."

With a soft laugh, Christina lifted Scott's and her linked
hands to kiss his, then held it against her cheek.

"This is promising," he said, and she released a breath.

"Had a surprise visit from my mother yesterday."

"Oh?"

"Don't you 'oh?' me. She said you'd been there."

"Busted."

"And how, exactly, did that come about?"

"I called Enid. Who was only too willing to help."

"I don't…oh. I guess I did give her my mother's contact
info in case of an emergency."

"And she and I both agreed this definitely qualified."

Christina rolled her eyes. "I think she likes you. My
mother, I mean. Don't think there's much question that
Enid likes you."

"You *think* your mother likes me?"

"You have to read between the lines with Mama. And what I read was...whatever you said must've lit one heck-uva fire under her butt. Not that things started out all that great, but...we began a dialogue, as they say. And kept it up until things started to make sense. And I realized..."

Christina lifted her eyes to Scott. "That she'd infected me with *her* issues. Put voices in my head. Voices that kept playing the same loop, over and over and over. Except... those voices lied, making me think..." Leaving the thought unfinished, she pulled her mouth into a straight line. "Not that I don't have my own demons to face down. My father did abandon me. As did Chris, at least emotionally. He was also very controlling, even if I didn't understand it at the time. But you're not Chris. Or my father. And it was hid-eously unfair of me to tar you with their brushes."

"Thank you."

"No, thank you, for...not giving up." One side of her mouth lifted. "For sticking to the plan."

"Who said there was a plan?"

She snorted. "Scott Fortune, you are the most focused person I have ever met. I seriously doubt you've ever let anything *just happen* from the time you could walk."

"And that's where you're wrong. Because I couldn't have planned your happening if my life depended on it. You, this," he said, gesturing to the landscape in front of them, "was part of something else's plan, believe me. All I did was...listen."

"Point taken. But still, once you got on board with that..." She grinned up at him again. "You took steps, right? It's okay, sweetpea—that's just who you are. Anyway, I got myself off track. About those voices..."

She tucked her good leg up underneath her, leaning more into him. "There are good voices, the ones that lead you forward. Then there are bad ones, that hold you back. That keep you afraid. Only what I realized was, those bad voices, they don't have any power unless you give it to them. Which is what I was doing. And I'm not anymore."

"Huh," Scott said, and Christina reared back to look at him.

"That's it? *Huh?*"

"Oh, trust me, there's plenty more. When you're finished."

Her gaze softened. "I do, actually."

"Do, what?"

"Trust you. Trust…whatever it is between us makes me *want* to trust you. Even if it makes no sense on the surface."

"Logic is highly overrated."

She laughed and snuggled closer. "So I'm beginning to figure out. But I finally got it through my head that it's like you said, that letting the past dictate my decisions, my *life,* is not only stupid, but counterproductive. I mean, there I was, yammering to all and sundry about all these plans I had to move forward, to become more than everyone thought I could be…but only as long as I could keep my heart locked up all nice and tight where nobody could get to it. And how dumb is that?"

"I assume that's a rhetorical question—?"

"Because that's what my mother was doing. Giving the past control. But you—" She sat up again. "Ohmigod," she said, her earnestness about to crack his heart in two, "you're the best thing that's ever happened to me! I'd be an idiot to turn that down because I'm afraid it won't last."

Scott shifted to cup her chin, hook her gaze in his. "You're still afraid this won't last?"

"Okay, so maybe *afraid's* not the right word. But it's not as if I can undo a lifetime of conditioning in a couple of days." She stroked her knuckles across his beard-shadowed cheek, the sensation making his mouth go dry. And, in all likelihood, his pupils dilate. "I do love you, Scott. With all my heart. But that heart's kinda bruised and battered, you know? I really *don't* know how to be loved. So I need time. And patience."

Gratitude and joy practically making him dizzy, Scott tucked her into his side again. Time, patience…those, he could give her.

"I know, honey. I do. That you can't always make something happen, no matter how right it feels." He let his fingers lazily track up and down her arm. "Take Blackie, for instance. The guy I bought him from really emphasized that you can't will somebody—or something—to trust you, that it has to be earned. By proving, over and over, you can be trusted. For as long as it takes." He paused, then said, "I was pushing you into something you weren't ready for, and I apologize. Even the house…if it's too much for you, if you don't think you could be comfortable here, I'll sell it and we'll find something else."

"But…you love this place."

He set her apart, only to take her face in his hands and lock their gazes. "I love you a helluva lot more, sweetheart. A house can never be my life. But you already are."

Now do you believe him?

Christina got up and crossed to the porch steps, wrapping one arm around the nearby column, feeling its strength seep into her very being. And with it, the last of the lies—that she was somehow less than, she had little to offer—finally dissipated.

This could all be yours, the voice whispered, *if you've got the cojones to accept it.*

The faith to believe you deserve it.

"I suppose I could get used to the house. In time."

Chuckling, Scott came up behind her to slip his arms around her waist.

Deserve him.

Because not only had she never been "less than," she was, and always had been, more than enough. For anybody. But especially for this man.

In whose fingers the ring sparkled. Hopefully.

Christina laughed. "You are one persistent cuss, aren'tcha?"

"That, or an idiot." He turned her around, one hand resting gently on her hip, the ring still between them. "There's a catch, though."

She pulled a face. "Your father, right?"

"Hardly. I swear, that will be a nonissue as soon as he meets you. After all, you charmed me, right?"

"I suppose that's true," she said, smiling, planting her hands on his strong, solid chest. "So what's this catch?"

"That we don't get a wedding band to go with this until you're good and ready. When you're as sure as I am, that this is no fairy tale. *This*—" his lips brushed hers "—is as real as it gets."

"I know," she whispered, holding out her hand so he could slip the ring back on her finger, where it belonged. Then she let him pull her into the circle of his arms...where she belonged.

Forever.

* * * * *

HEART & HOME

Heartwarming romances where love can
happen right when you least expect it.

SPECIAL EDITION

COMING NEXT MONTH
AVAILABLE JANUARY 31, 2012

#2167 FORTUNE'S VALENTINE BRIDE
The Fortunes of Texas: Whirlwind Romance
Marie Ferrarella

#2168 THE RETURN OF BOWIE BRAVO
Bravo Family Ties
Christine Rimmer

#2169 JACKSON HOLE VALENTINE
Rx for Love
Cindy Kirk

#2170 A MATCH MADE BY CUPID
The Foster Brothers
Tracy Madison

#2171 ALMOST A HOMETOWN BRIDE
Helen R. Myers

#2172 HIS MOST IMPORTANT WIN
Cynthia Thomason

You can find more information on upcoming Harlequin® titles,
free excerpts and more at www.HarlequinInsideRomance.com.

HSECNM0112

REQUEST YOUR FREE BOOKS!

2 FREE NOVELS PLUS 2 FREE GIFTS!

Harlequin

SPECIAL EDITION

Life, Love & Family

Discover a touching new trilogy from
USA TODAY bestselling author

Janice Kay Johnson

Between Love and Duty

As the eldest brother of three, Duncan MacLachlan
is used to being in control and maintaining an
emotional distance; as a police captain it's his job.
But when he meets Jane Brooks, Duncan soon finds
his control slipping away. Together, they fight for a
young boy's future, and soon Duncan finds himself
hoping to build a future with Jane.

Available February 2012

From Father to Son
(March 2012)

The Call of Bravery
(April 2012)

*Louisa Morgan loves being around children.
So when she has the opportunity to tutor bedridden Ellie,
she's determined to bring joy back into the motherless
girl's world. Can she also help Ellie's father open his
heart again? Read on for a sneak peek of*

THE COWBOY FATHER

*by Linda Ford,
available February 2012 from Love Inspired Historical.*

Why had Louisa thought she could do this job? A bubble of self-pity whispered she was totally useless, but Louisa ignored it. She wasn't useless. She could help Ellie if the child allowed it.

Emmet walked her out, waiting until they were out of earshot to speak. "I sense you and Ellie are not getting along."

"Ellie has lost her freedom. On top of that, everything is new. Familiar things are gone. Her only defense is to exert what little independence she has left. I believe she will soon tire of it and find there are more enjoyable ways to pass the time."

He looked doubtful. Louisa feared he would tell her not to return. But after several seconds' consideration, he sighed heavily. "You're right about one thing. She's lost everything. She can hardly be blamed for feeling out of sorts."

"She hasn't lost everything, though." Her words were quiet, coming from a place full of certainty that Emmet was more than enough for this child. "She has you."

"She'll always have me. As long as I live." He clenched his fists. "And I fully intend to raise her in such a way that even if something happened to me, she would never feel like I was gone. I'd be in her thoughts and in her actions

SHLIHEXP0212

every day."

Peace filled Louisa. "Exactly what my father did."

Their gazes connected, forged a single thought about fathers and daughters…how each needed the other. How sweet the relationship was.

Louisa tipped her head away first. "I'll see you tomorrow."

Emmet nodded. "Until tomorrow then."

She climbed behind the wheel of their automobile and turned toward home. She admired Emmet's devotion to his child. It reminded her of the love her own father had lavished on Louisa and her sisters. Louisa smiled as fond memories of her father filled her thoughts. Ellie was a fortunate child to know such love.

Louisa understands what both father and daughter are going through. Will her compassion help them heal—and form a new family? Find out in
THE COWBOY FATHER
by Linda Ford, available February 14, 2012.

Love Inspired Books celebrates 15 years of inspirational romance in 2012! February puts the spotlight on Love Inspired Historical, with each book celebrating family and the special place it has in our hearts. Be sure to pick up all four Love Inspired Historical stories, available February 14, wherever books are sold.